There was no sound, not even birds, nor insects humming. Everything was preternaturally still. *It looks like a scene from a movie,* a little voice said.

The hairs on the back of my neck began to rise.

"Tracy, come back!" I called. And then, as she didn't stop, I opened my own door and jumped out. I ran toward her, reaching her just a few steps from the too-thick shrubbery that could so easily be concealing a crouching figure.

I reached her, grabbed her, jerked her back and away. And then, just as I flung her past me towards the car, I heard a great crack as though the sky had split. The heavens turned red, and I went down into fire and darkness.

point

A TOUCH OF MADNESS

Lavinia Harris

SCHOLASTIC INC.
New York Toronto London Auckland Sydney

Library of Congress Cataloging in Publication Data

Harris, Lavinia.
    A touch of madness.

    Summary: Josh and his girlfriend Sidney, teenage
partners in computer investigation, track down a
gang attempting to sabotage a company by using its
new computer game for gambling.
    [1. Computers—Fiction. 2. Mystery and detective
stories] I. Title.
PZ7.H24212To   1985   [Fic]   85–2268
ISBN 0-590-33057-8

ISBN 0-590-33057-8

12 11 10 9 8 7 6 5 4 3 2 1   9   5 6 7 8 9/8 0/9

                Printed in the U.S.A.   01

A TOUCH
OF MADNESS

Chapter 1

It was on a balmy evening in early April that our involvement in the fiendish plot began. That's how a text-adventure computer game would begin, so I might as well, too, since it's appropriate. Sidney Scott Webster IV (that's me), owner/president of SSW Enterprises, *Computer Consultants* (Discretion guaranteed) and Joshua J. Rivington III, my (I *mean* SSW's) computer genius/rationalist/chauvinist were celebrating SSW's latest triumph.

Spring vacation was a week away, and with it a free trip to a Silicon Valley, California, computer show (compliments of SMN Computers, for whom we're testing out a *very* special new product). We'd just received a fat, fat check from the sponsor of the soap opera my Aunt Jane produces — payment officially for SSW's computerized market research, and unofficially for detective work that had solved a nasty crime.

We had dined at Lakeland, New Jersey's

fanciest restaurant (compliments of SSW's expense account). We had followed that by a jazz concert at the university auditorium (compliments of Josh). We had now progressed to the couch in the SSW Enterprises office, formerly the Webster family room, where we were making up for lost time and feeling mellow.

Not that Josh put it that way. "Exploring the options" was what he called it, between nibbling my ear and doing some other exploring I won't go into here. Josh may be different in such ways as wearing three-piece business suits (to school yet!) and looking down his nose at school athletics, but fortunately he's not so different when it comes to basic matters. Hence the couch. Hence my murmuring demurely into one of *his* ears, "Just business, huh? Try explaining that to my dad, when he walks in. My folks are due home any minute."

"Dr. Webster never walks into a business office without knocking. He's too professional," Josh said. Nonetheless, he straightened his tie — with his left hand, so he didn't have to take his right arm from around me. "I have something to talk to you about, Webster. While we're still alone. Relative to the California trip."

"We've been alone all evening," I pointed out. "And if you're going to drop any bomb 'relative to the California trip,' you'd *better* do it while we're alone. My mother's still dubious about our going. On our own. Together. With somebody else paying for it."

"Nonsense," Josh said airily. "It's not a pleasure trip —"

"Ha!"

"It's computer business. Sam Kennedy's not paying for it; his company is, on account of we're testing out Samantha for him."

Samantha, the third member of our computer investigation team, is a trial model, temperamental, SMN Gemini computer, who can do everything including read people's minds. Well, mine, anyway.

"We're not even staying in a hotel, for Pete's sake. We're staying with the Kennedys. And Sam Kennedy's an old Vietnam Special Forces buddy of Thor Jorgensen, who's not only our high school science teacher, but your dad's research partner. What's for your mother to get worked up about?"

"What, indeed?" I asked mischievously, wiping lip gloss off Josh's cheek. Josh reddened. One of the endearing things about Joshua J. Rivington III — Mr. Supercool — is that he still blushes when he catches himself feeling human emotions like the rest of us.

I should explain that Joshua J. Rivington III, in addition to arrogance, an engineer-type brain, the three-piece suits, and his trademark boots that add an inch or so of height, also has crisply curly black hair, dark eyes you'd die for, and drive he intends will make him a millionaire before he's thirty. And, I must admit, there's nothing wrong with his physique either, even if it does come from fencing, archery, and the more esoteric martial arts, rather than from football, basketball, and baseball to which our neighborhood computer jocks are addicted.

Me, I'm a high school sophomore: small, dark-eyed, light brown hair. Looks that make strong men melt (which is nice) but also make them not take me seriously (which isn't). I'm beginning to find, though, that being small and fluffy can be a very convenient protective covering. Anyway, *Josh* takes me seriously. I had doubts for a while about the melting effect where he was concerned, but not anymore.

Ever since Josh and I first ran into each other (literally!) there's been *something* going on between the two of us. Correction: the *three* of us. Have you ever tried being one corner of a triangle composed of male, female, and computer? Not that Samantha's just any computer. Samantha (official title: SMN Gemini prototype test-model #1) is a personality. For starters, she can talk back, she can send and receive via alpha-state brain waves, and a whole lot more. But she wasn't giving me any competition tonight!

A small smile tugged my mouth, but I slid off the couch and pinned my hair back up. "You said you wanted to talk. So talk."

Josh cleared his throat. "I've been thinking about what your dad said to us when that soaps check came in. About how we're starting to make real money, and we need to make plans so we won't blow it."

"Like adding a tenth computer to the nine already in your collection? Or buying that laser printer you've been eyeing?"

"Cut it out. I'm serious. Your dad's right, we can't just let this kind of cash sit around earning minimum amounts of interest, like I've been doing up to now. Only because I've been too busy to map out a real strategy," he added hastily. I grinned to myself. Strategy and statistics are meat and drink to Josh. "I need to make my cash *make* money for me, if I want to pay for Harvard Business School."

"Right after you've sailed through your undergraduate work in two years at most?" I asked innocently.

"I *said* be serious. I've taken all but a couple of hundred dollars out of my college savings and bought a large block of stock in Unicorn Unlimited."

I stared at him. "You *what*?"

"Bought stock in Unicorn Unlimited. That's the company that's cleaning up with all those computer games —"

"I know what Unicorn is," I interrupted. "I'm just . . . flabbergasted. I didn't think you'd ever played a computer game in your life."

"You don't have to play the stupid things," Josh said loftily, "to know they're one of the hottest things on the retail market. They're addictive — to people whose minds run that way. Unicorn's in the computer industry, which I do know something about, after all. And it's a very sound investment; the *Wall Street Journal* says so. Besides, I checked out the head of Unicorn. Jeremy Tyler's a mathematician. Statistician. Graduated from Harvard's grad school of business with honors when he was twenty."

In other words, Tyler was everything Josh fancied himself as, I thought, vastly entertained. "Why are you telling me all this?" I inquired. "If you're trying to sell me Unicorn stock, don't bother. Mother's handling my money for me. She's a mathematician, too." I looked at him slantwise from underneath my lashes. "If you're laying your hand and heart and bankbook at my feet, (1) I'm only sixteen, and (2) isn't it my father you should be talking finances with?"

"Will you shut up and listen? You know it will be at least ten years before I'm established enough in a career for us to —" Josh stopped abruptly and turned bright red. "What I'm trying to say," he went on with dignity, "is that I've put a block of the stock I just bought in your name."

"You *what*?"

"Put it in your name. Because I think it's an investment you should be in on, and because I was fairly sure I couldn't persuade you to buy. What I wasn't sure of was how you'd react — or your father."

"He'll turn purple," I said at last, carefully. "Then he'll tell you it is your money and you shouldn't be spending that amount of it on me. And my mother will tell you it's not . . . appropriate."

Josh snorted. "This is the twentieth century, not the nineteenth. And I wouldn't have all that money if it hadn't been for you and SSW. As you've never been exactly shy about pointing out, I was making a royal mess out of being self-employed."

"Not because you're not good with computing. Or with the business end of business. Just with —"

"I know, I know." Josh cut me off before I could say *with scheduling; with pacing himself; with people.* "The point is, you and SSW have been good for . . . my career. I *want* you to have some of the stock I bought. The thing is, can you persuade your folks —"

We heard the roar of a car outside our windows. "I think *you'll* have a chance to try persuading them," I was just saying, when the doorbell rang imperiously. I jumped. "Good grief, don't tell me they both forgot their keys!"

I ran down the seven steps to the main floor, straightening my rumpled dress as I did so. Josh followed. Only it wasn't my parents on the doorstep. It was Lakeland's preeminent computer jocks. Charles Gordon Richardson, alias Ceegee (scarecrow-type, next-door neighbor) walked right in, waving computer game boxes in the air. He was followed by his good buddy, Steve Wiczniewski (senior, star athlete), similarly encumbered.

Trailing behind them was Steve's girl and my best friend, dark-haired Cordelia Quinn. She was carrying nothing but a look of embarrassment.

"We saw the lights on in your office," Ceegee said happily. "We've been over at Paramus Park Mall, and I've finally gotten a copy of *Numero Uno*. After I've had my name on the list for it for months! I knew you guys would want to try it. Hi, Rivington!" He charged for the stairs. Steve and Josh followed.

I caught Cordelia by the arm. "I'll kill you for this," I murmured meaningfully.

"I tried to stop them," Cordelia muttered back. "You didn't want me to tell them *why* they wouldn't be wanted, did you? By the way, your hair is falling down."

I blushed, and ducked into the downstairs bathroom to repair my disheveled state, and when I went back up to "Sidney's level" of our split-level house, all the romantic mood that had been there was gone.

Steve was sprawled comfortably on the old blue-and-beige rug while a music video blared on MTV. CeeGee had loaded *Numero Uno*, Unicorn's fabulous new game, into Dad's old Apple and was already zipping through it with delight. Josh occupied his favorite easy chair, looking sardonic.

"Why anyone with half a brain wants to waste time and money on computerized gameplaying. . . ." he murmured. Ceegee looked injured.

"Come off it, Rivington! Have you ever even *tried* a computer game? The main reason I bought this one was because of you. No, I mean it," he said to the room at large, as Steve jeered. "Rivington gave me a long lecture in the locker room today about how I should stash my college money in something that would give me more profit. Like investments. I know a lot about computers and computer games, but I don't know beans about investments, so I figured *Numero Uno* was a painless way to learn. It's about making money on the stock market, after all."

"Learn? From a game?" Josh scoffed.

"Don't knock it till you've tried it," Cordelia answered tartly.

"I should think anyone would want firsthand experience in a field before getting mixed up in it financially," I said, innocently, to the ceiling. Josh shot me a daggers look.

"Hey, is Rivington thinking of going into games programming?" Steve asked with interest.

"I'm sure I could if I wanted to," Josh said shortly. He took the seat Ceegee elaborately vacated, and squinted at the screen. "Hmmm," he said. There was a silence, while he keyboarded.

"Hmmmm?" I said at last, when I could stand the suspense no more.

"What? Oh. This isn't so feeble after all," Josh said bemusedly. "Good underlying logic and statistics. Of course, it was written by a Harvard math wizard," he added quickly as the others jeered. "Maybe I will look into game programming. People are making megabucks at it, so I hear."

The clock struck midnight. Josh spun around and flipped the TV channel selector off of MTV. "Business news show coming on. I want to check on my college investments," he apologized absently as Steve yelped. *Josh might look down on computer game addicts, but he showed all the signs of becoming a stock market addict,* I thought, amused.

We were treated to a picture of talking heads. At first I couldn't hear what they were saying, because the others were wrangling with ribald laughter in the background. Then two words rang out.

". . . Unicorn Unlimited. . . ."

"Shut up!" Josh shouted, sharp and unexpected. All of a sudden the room was very silent. So silent, we could hear the newswoman's voice loud and clear.

". . . price of Unicorn Unlimited stock plummeted sharply following confiscation by the Dade County, Florida, district attorney of all *Numero Uno* games being offered for sale within the county. The move followed raids by Dade County law enforcement officers last evening on a Florida syndicate that was using the Unicorn Unlimited game as the basis of an illegal gambling operation. Police would reveal little other than that the roundup was 'the result of intense police surveillance following an anonymous tip,' but Dade County sources hint the Florida gambling operation is tied to major organized crime. As rumors that a 'restraint of trade' order may be filed against Unicorn Unlimited spread through the financial world. . . ."

As the rumors had spread, Josh's college savings — *all* Josh's college savings — had in this one day diminished by a third.

Chapter 2

"Gambling? With *Numero Uno*?" Ceegee inquired with interest.

Josh snapped, "Just shut up." Not nastily, just as if he was on automatic pilot. He never took his eyes off the TV screen. I never took my eyes off Josh.

If the others knew Josh's loss — and its seriousness — they would freak out. If Josh didn't freak out, it was only because he wouldn't let himself.

Cordelia looked at me, and her lips framed the words, *What's wrong?*

Not now, I signaled back, and Cordelia nodded imperceptibly. "I think it's time we got going and left these two alone. My folks will kill me. I swore I'd be home by midnight. Talk to you, Sidney." She made for the stairs, and Steve and Ceegee obediently followed, taking their computer games.

I let them let themselves out. In the empty house, Josh and I faced each other.

"Unicorn will make out all right." The

words rang tinnily in my own ears. "*Numero Uno* just came out, and it's selling like mad. You said so."

Josh didn't answer. He was snapping through TV channels till he found an all-night news show. Within minutes, Unicorn Unlimited's name came up. This time it was being covered as feature news, and the news was hot. A congressional committee investigating organized gambling was subpoenaing Unicorn Unlimited's sales records. It was also going to hear testimony from one Aldous P. Shuttleworth, president of a group called Advocates for Children, who had held a press conference this afternoon and charged that Unicorn games were deliberately designed for gambling purposes and were therefore dangerous to children.

"It's crazy," I said in bewilderment. "It's just plain crazy. Gambling? In kids' *computer games*?"

"Wake up, Webster!" Josh said harshly. "Gambling's a fact of life. And it isn't a case of children's toys. Unicorn games are big business! And not just for kids. You heard the jokes. What was crazy was *me*, taking a gamble with my college money."

He snapped the TV set off with finality, thrust his hands deep in his pockets, and paced. "This is what I get for violating my own rules. Buying on impulse. Without doing sufficient research. Because—" he stopped abruptly.

I could complete the sentence. Because the

size of the checks we'd just gotten had thrown him off his cherished balance. Because he had an image of himself as a financial wizard. Because he wanted to impress me — to provide for me.

The fact that he was even facing those scalding truths, with or without verbalizing them, spoke volumes.

There was a look in Josh's eyes that frightened me. It was more than discouraged, or angry. It was hopeless. Full of self-flagellation. Un-Josh. I ran to him and hugged him hard.

"The Unicorn stock will bounce back. You have ages of time before you'll need the money."

"Not if I start college this fall, the way I planned to," Josh said bleakly.

"Josh, listen to me! Investing the money *was* a smart move." I didn't say I thought putting all his eggs in one basket had been pretty dumb. I pulled back to arms' length, still holding him, and looked him squarely in the eye. "I know one thing. You're taking back that stock you put in my name. It won't make up all the money you've lost, but it will go part way."

"I wanted you to have it," Josh said, not moving.

I couldn't say I didn't need it. I couldn't say my father was a surgeon, and hospital chief of staff, and could put me through college with no help from me. I couldn't point out that Josh's father was dead, and his mother

didn't have money, and that unlike me he'd
have to pay his own way. Instead I hugged
him. And then I kissed him, and then I just
held him, motionless, for a long long time.
Until we heard my parents' car in the driveway and Josh disengaged himself, moving as
though he were drugged.

"I don't want to talk to them. Not now."
He kissed me — *hard* — and then hurried
downstairs and out the back way, while my
parents were still coming in from the garage.

I wanted to run to them, but I didn't. I went
to bed, and lay awake in the dark, while
images of the evening, that had begun so
beautifully, moved inexorably through my
head.

In the morning, before I was even out of
bed, Cordelia phoned. "What's the matter?
I know something is."

"You heard that stuff last night about
Unicorn Unlimited? Josh put all his college
money into it."

"Ohhh," Cordelia said comprehensively.
And then, in uncanny repetition of my own
thoughts, "What are you going to do about
it? You're going to investigate Unicorn and
the Advocates for Children, aren't you?
You're computer detectives, after all."

"You think there's something fishy, do
you?"

"So fishy it stinks," Cordelia said graphi-
cally. "You know our school. It's a Class A
rumor mill, and kids have been matching
pennies and playing card games for lunch

money, if they could get away with it, since fourth grade. I haven't heard a *word* about Unicorn games and gambling before this. Neither have Steve or Ceegee."

"What about this Advocates for Children group?"

"That I've heard about. Mom's on their mailing list, probably because she subscribes to magazines on how to bring up kids. It's one of those groups that wants to protect kids from harsh reality, preferably by turning the clock back to the nineteenth century. I've heard them on the subject of comic books and music videos, but never on computer games before."

"Quite a coincidence they called a press conference the same day that the sheriff's department holds a gambling raid."

"Isn't it?" Cordelia agreed dryly. "Look, if we can do any help with hacking or research, holler, will you?"

"I will. Promise you won't let Josh know I've told you. He'd probably kill me." I hung up and went downstairs to do something else for which he'd kill me — tell my parents.

Dad had gone out already, but my mother was there, taking a cinnamon-fragrant coffee cake from the oven. "Sit down and tell me what's wrong. I know something is. The house was too still when we got home last night. I couldn't believe Josh had already torn himself away."

"Something's wrong, but not between Josh and me." I sat down and, while Mother pushed a glass of orange juice toward me and poured coffee, I poured the whole thing out.

"Something's queer. It's all happening . . . too fast, and too loud."

"Things can happen that way. Especially in high-tech industries," Mother said. "When something happens that can affect the company's profits, people sell out quickly and the price of the stock goes down. Obviously, that's happening now."

"I know all that. What I want to know is *why*."

"Are you forgetting the power of publicity?" Mother asked me wryly. "News of that gambling raid in Florida hit the airwaves yesterday morning. You didn't know because you'd already left for school. You and Josh went out for dinner before the early news came on last night, and I don't suppose either one of you looked at an evening newspaper. By the way, Unicorn's all over the front pages of *The New York Times* this morning."

I looked, and beheld two fascinating pictures. One of the gambling raid, the other of Aldous P. Shuttleworth, looking like a genial beardless Santa, brandishing a Unicorn Unlimited game. The kitchen, with its polished wood and copper, its fireplace and friendly rocking chair, was tranquil and soothing, but I felt a chill. I pushed my cup somberly over to Mother for a refill.

"This Advocates for Children group has become very vocal lately," Mother said thoughtfully. "Mr. Shuttleworth's been turning up on talk shows regularly. He believes children should be protected from harmful influences, and he has a lot of supporters."

"Hence a lot of votes. Hence the congressional hearing."

"Sidney, stop it. These people are very serious, and they're sincere. There *are* a lot of harmful influences in the world today, and you know it." Mother eyed me. "It seems to me I remember you losing your allowance to Ceegee in a card game once when you were little. I also remember neither you nor your father and I were very thrilled."

I blushed. "Have you heard Mr. Shuttleworth say anything about Unicorn games before this?" I asked quickly. Mother shook her head.

"Not till now. Of course, there's always been criticism that video games have a hypnotic, almost drug-like effect in large doses. On the other hand, I've also heard somewhere that blasting space invaders with those silly little laser guns can increase the players' reflex and motor skills." Mother regarded me thoughtfully. "One good thing for Josh's sake," she said casually. "This is Saturday. Nothing happens over a weekend in the financial world. Maybe by Monday things will have calmed down and Josh's Unicorn stock will be worth a bit more again."

Maybe. Josh could probably quote statistics on the probability, but I didn't think they'd be much comfort to him right now.

I didn't hear from Josh all day, though I stayed near the phone in case he called. By late afternoon I was feeling frantic. Finally I picked up the phone. There was no answer at Josh's apartment. That didn't necessarily mean he wasn't home; only that his mother wasn't. I thought hard, and then I took a deep breath and walked over there.

The Rivingtons live in a small garden apartment near the center of town. I rang, and when Josh didn't answer I backed off and looked up at his window. It was open to the April breeze, and I could see his head in silhouette. So I hollered.

Josh looked, and came down to the door to let me in. "I meant to call you. I've been on the computer all day." His eyes looked strained and red, as though he hadn't slept. He stood back, and I went past him up the stairs.

"In my room," Josh said, and I followed.

Josh's room, which he uses as an office, is small and Spartan: bed shoved against the wall as a couch, almost all other space occupied by shelves and file cabinets and his nine (count 'em, nine) computers. Everything lined up with meticulous precision, engineer-neat. That is, usually. I stood in the middle of the room, looked around, and blinked.

"Sorry about that," Josh said wearily, sweeping long trails of printouts off the bed's Navajo blanket, so I could sit down. "I've been trying to calculate Unicorn's chances of recovery, and college costs, and whether I should bail out of Unicorn while I can still salvage anything."

Only it wasn't Unicorn Unlimited statistics, or college budgets, that were showing on his SMN Capricorn's screen. It was *Numero Uno*. *Numero Uno* printouts were draped across chair and bookshelves, like toilet paper in trees on Halloween.

"I don't believe it," I said slowly.

Josh reddened. "I went out and bought a copy so I could find out just what nasty stuff Shuttleworth claims is in it. Actually, the game isn't as juvenile as I'd expected."

He didn't meet my eyes. Rivington, the superior skeptic, was getting hooked. The corners of my mouth twitched, but I controlled them sternly. "Did you find anything to do with gambling?"

"Zilch, no matter what combination of answers I try. And I've tried plenty."

"Forget about the game itself for now. And forget about bailing out," I said briefly. "At least till we get the answers to some questions."

"If you mean about what's happening to Unicorn, that's painfully obvious, isn't it?"

"I know *what's* happening. What *I* want to know is *why*? How come that Mr. Shuttleworth just happened to find gambling characteristics in *Numero Uno*, and called a press conference to announce it, the same day a sheriff's department in another state staged a gambling raid? For one thing, I wouldn't have thought Mr. Shuttleworth would recognize gambling characteristics when he saw them, if there weren't dice and chips on a table. For another thing, how come that sheriff's department got an anonymous tip? And from whom? Mother says there's never been a hint of a tie-in between gambling and children's computer games before. Why the suggestion that Unicorn deliberately created their games for illegal use? They're making millions out of their games without it. And why did Unicorn stock crash so far so fast, right after it's been so much in demand? It's almost as if somebody had inside knowledge."

Josh looked at me with respect. "That's the first sensible explanation I've heard so far." I could see his mental wheels start turning. "It could all be coincidence, or it could be coincidence had a little help. Who's apt to know something about what's going on in the software industry?"

"*We* will, next week. Are you forgetting we're going to that Silicon Valley computer show? We're bound to find out things. Maybe we'll even get to meet that Jeremy Tyler."

Josh didn't look at me. "I've been thinking about the California trip. I don't think I should go. I can probably pick up some free-lance programming to do during vacation time. That will help my college situation some."

"Are you out of your mind? You have to go! That computer show's our only lead to getting a handle on this case!"

There, I'd said it. Josh's eyebrow lifted. " 'Our'? 'Case'?"

"Definitely case. And definitely ours. We're supposed to be such hotshot detectives, aren't we? Some hotshots if we can't salvage your money by salvaging Unicorn! Everything's just . . . too coincidental; it would be driving me crazy even if you weren't involved. But you are. So *I* am."

It was as simple as that. And as complicated.

I threw in the clinchers. "If you don't go to California, I won't. I don't think my folks would let me go alone, anyway. And you said you bought some of that Unicorn stock for me. Are you going to let it go down the drain without us fighting for it?"

Josh smiled faintly. "I don't suppose there's a fraction of probability you'd stay out of the fight?"

"Not a hoot in hell," I agreed gravely. "You don't need a computer to tell you that. So don't waste your time trying."

But I knew, even as he hugged me, that more than money had been lost last night. Josh's fierce independence, and pride, and humiliation, rose like a wall between us. I was in his arms, but we were further apart than we'd been in a long, long time.

Chapter 3

Early Friday afternoon, Josh and I boarded a plane for California at Newark Airport. I was wearing my hair up, my Easter suit, and high heels. My attache case with the special security locks, a gift from Dad, was tucked beneath my feet. Josh was attired in navy-blue pinstripes, no less, and his best boots.

Samantha was with us, too. Her standard-issue, easily-replaceable parts were in the baggage hold. Her brain — her special operating system, and her special programs — was in Josh's largest attache case, balanced on his knees. Sam Kennedy, her inventor, wanted to check her out. We would have brought her, anyway.

Ever since the invitation for this trip had come, I'd been imagining how it would be to take off into the wild blue yonder with Josh beside me. Suffice it to say, reality was not like my rosy dreams. Josh was somber, wrapped in a shroud of preoccupation, and though he held my hand as we took off, he seldom spoke. I flitted between awareness and that half-awake, tuned-into-the-subconscious that Dad calls alpha state. I closed my eyes, and the bits and pieces of the past week unscrolled on the monitor screen of my mind and took on shape and form.

Without telling Josh, Cordelia and I had done some research into other crusades similar to the Advocates for Children's new one against Unicorn games. Some past campaigns succeeded in closing down their targets legally, and some did not. But one thing had almost universally occurred. For a short time or long, the attacks had been bad for business.

The members of these activist groups were mostly decent, sincerely motivated people. But that did not necessarily mean no one was capitalizing on their efforts for less unselfish purposes. Was anything like that involved now?

On Tuesday, Jeremy Tyler, the president of Unicorn, had been notified he must testify before the congressional committee on gambling some time soon. TV gave a lot of attention to the government's announcement, to Tyler's reaction, and to Aldous P. Shuttleworth's comments on both of the above.

By Wednesday, the value of Unicorn stock had dropped so low that the authorities suspended trading in it.

All week TV had kept harping on the story. There were tantalizing snippets on the Florida gambling raids, on organized crime figures denying their involvement, on Advocates for Children planning an intensive lobbying campaign to have Unicorn's games permanently taken off the market. Mr. Shuttleworth looked more grieved than angry, but some of the members of his group were breathing fire and threatening direct action, which kind of scared me.

My mind kept churning this way and that, and by the time we were over the middle of the country my brain was getting tired.

"What trance were you off in?" Josh inquired over our airplane meal.

"You don't want to know."

"Unicorn?" Our eyes met. "Me, too," Josh said heavily. Then he deliberately changed the subject, and for the rest of the trip we spoke of Unicorn Unlimited no more.

We landed in late afternoon, California time — the middle of the evening by our body clocks. We retrieved our suitcases at the baggage carousel, and were rounding up Samantha's various boxes when a voice behind us said, "SSW, I presume?"

I whirled around, and Josh straightened.

A tall man with thinning tan hair came loping toward us, holding out his hand. "You must be Sidney Webster and Joshua Rivington. I'm Sam Kennedy. Make it Sam." He was California-casual in open-neck sports shirt and comfortably shabby slacks, and reminded me of nothing so much as an amiable stork. It was hard to realize he was a genius, and a millionaire.

"How did you recognize us?" I asked.

Sam smiled. "I was told to watch for a three-piece suit and boots. Got everything? Here's a luggage cart. My wife's waiting for us in a no-parking zone out front."

I had to hurry to keep up, his legs were so long, and Josh was always brisk. I was about to make an acid comment, by way of light conversation, when my eyes beheld the vehicle awaiting us, and I fell speechless.

Sam Kennedy *was* a millionaire, in a high-tech glamour field. I might have known he'd have a high-tech car. It was a sedate tan, but that was deceptive. It was a Mercedes. A *stretched* Mercedes, and there was an admiring little crowd hanging around to ogle. Jennifer Kennedy, behind the wheel, was equally spectacular. She was slim and tanned, with shiring shoulder-length dark brown hair that matched her eyes. Her silk suit was set off with gold jewelry that was heavy, simple, striking.

"You ride up front with me, Sidney," she invited. "We'll let the boys play with the gadgets in the back." I slid in beside her, my eyes widening as I saw the dashboard. Jennifer noticed it, and chuckled.

"You didn't think a Silicon Valley tinkerer could let a car alone, did you? Wait till you get a good look at the back seat's glories! Sam can run his whole company out of this mobile office, and often does." She touched buttons, and the car purred off, literally, into the sunset.

Steve and Ceegee are always falling in love with cars, to my amused incomprehension. This car, *I* could love, and as for Josh — I stole a backward glance — clearly, it was infatuation at first sight. The outside was built like an armored tank, and the inside was a glove leather-upholstered cocoon. There was a telephone, of course. There was a stereo, a TV with a VCR. There was a bar stocked with the diet soda that Sam drank like water. There was a computer that, like Samantha, talked.

"It's another Gemini test model, like the one you're using. This one doesn't have tele-pathic communication, though," Sam said, grinning. "I thought that could be distracting in a car. Suppose it read my mind while I was daydreaming about Mexico, when I was really trying to get transported to the office."

"You don't mean the computer steers the car!" Josh said.

"It can, but the Department of Motor Vehicles and I won't let it," Jennifer said firmly.

Sam laughed. "She won't let me drive, either," he confided. "I'm too apt to go off in a creative trance! Fortunately, I'd rather sit in the back with the computer than behind the wheel. I have a regular driver, and when he's not on call, Jennifer drives. The seats open down into beds, and there's a miniature stove and refrigerator built into the back, for camping. Maybe we can take you kids out in the desert for a few days while you're here."

"If there's time." There was an odd note in Jennifer's voice.

"What I really want to see is the SMN headquarters," Josh spoke up. "The assembly line, and your research and development department, if you'll let us."

"Considering you're testing Gemini #1 for us, I think we can trust you," Sam said dryly. But there was that same kind of double-edged tone in his voice, also. Josh's eyes and mine locked.

"The computer show," I said. "When does it start?"

"For the public, Sunday," Sam replied. "There's a special preview Saturday evening, a fund-raiser for the valley's new mental health clinic. A lot of dignitaries, industry people, and important customers are coming to it. And the press, of course. Several of the exhibitors will be entertaining."

"SMN?" I asked.

"We're hosting a Sunday morning brunch at one of the hotels where customers are staying, and a buffet dinner after the preview Sunday. We may have a party at the house some time in the week — if no crisis pops up to conflict," Jennifer said. There was a strained expression on her face.

"Jennifer's a lawyer," Sam explained, "specializing in the computer industry." He sounded preoccupied. I stole a look in the rearview mirror, and intercepted an exchange of glances between the Kennedys. I could feel Josh's eyes suddenly boring into me through the back of my bucket seat.

The sky to the west was now flamingo-color. Sam waved a lanky arm. "The entrance to the SMN plant is just ahead."

"Could we stop and see it?" Josh asked promptly.

Jennifer spoke up before Sam could answer. "Won't that keep till tomorrow? You must both be tired and hungry —"

"We ate on the plane," Josh interrupted. I could have killed him. My antennas, as he liked to call them, were picking up all kinds of vibes, and here was Josh riding roughshod over them. I turned to Jennifer and smiled.

"What do *you* think we ought to do?"

"That depends on what you two feel like. We could stop at a restaurant for a leisurely dinner. Or give you the half-hour jet-paced tour of SMN and then have a snack. Or. . . ."

Her voice quickened, and I knew this was what she really wanted. "We could go straight home, and Sam will throw some fresh crabs on the grill. If you aren't too tired, there are a couple of people I'd like to have come meet you: one of my clients, Jeremy Tyler, and his sister Tracy.

From the back seat, I heard Josh's suddenly indrawn breath.

Chapter 4

"I'd love to meet them," I said promptly. There was no way we could let this opportunity slip by.

"*You* call Jeremy," Jennifer said to Sam.

I couldn't help myself; I turned around in my seat. There were things going on underneath their words that needed consideration, and I could tell Josh thought so, too. Sam regarded Jennifer thoughtfully for a long minute. Then he punched a button and said aloud, "Locate Jeremy Tyler."

On the computer's control panel, red and green lights like Samantha's started dancing. "New Gemini feature. No booting up necessary," Sam murmured, seeing Josh and me react. "The computer just goes into a kind of sleep till it's activated by button or by voice command. Or in the model you're using, by telepathy. I'll install one of the new chips in yours tomorrow."

"*Connection made,*" sang the computer, and Sam picked up the telephone receiver.

"Jeremy? Sam. Where are you, home? We're throwing shellfish on the grill. You and that kid sister of yours come over. . . . Jer, I insist. It will be better if you do get out. . . . Well, hog-tie her if you have to! We'll look for you in thirty minutes. See you."

The Mercedes swung into a drive lined with old gnarled trees. "Welcome to computer heaven," Sam said. "Or the other extreme, depending on your point of view."

The house looked as if it had crouched there on its hillside for a thousand years. The walls were adobe and the roof and floors were terra-cotta tile. We went inside through a heavy carved old door, and only then did it begin to dawn on me what a lot of money, as well as thought and love, had gone into this house.

There were squooshy sofas covered in homespun or tawny leather. There were low-slung tooled leather chairs. The rugs could have been American Indian, or Turkish, or from the Caucasus, I wasn't sure. I did know it was very, very low-keyed, and very comfortable. Electronics were so well concealed I didn't notice them till Jennifer touched what looked like a copper panel on the wall, and things started happening.

The lights went on. So did soft music. So did an enormous projection TV, with the evening news. Aldous P. Shuttleworth was holding forth on the evils of Unicorn games.

For an instant I was very conscious of everyone's expression. Jennifer, deeply worried. Josh, as if he'd received a sharp jolt back to reality. Sam — for the first time, I realized he could lose his California calm — snapped, "Turn that damn thing off." At the same moment, a dignified Mexican woman with black coronet braids appeared and Sam's face softened to a smile.

"Sidney Webster, Josh Rivington — Mrs. Eufemia Gallego, the person who makes our impossible lifestyle possible. We're eating in after all, Eufemia. I'll do the cooking."

"I made some guacamole and gazpacho, and I picked up some figs and things. I'll see you in the morning, then. Mike will have the car around at eight, unless you notify him to come earlier." She flashed a brilliant smile at all of us, and withdrew.

"Make yourselves at home," Sam invited. "Would you like to kibitz while I do the crabs, or sack out for a while, or see the house?"

"I'd love to see the house," I said quickly. Jennifer led the way, and I followed, with Josh bringing up the rear.

The house was basically one-story, but it rambled casually up and down different levels. My bedroom had a fireplace and a wrought-iron balcony that reached out into one of the huge gnarled trees.

"Sam and I are at the end, here," Jennifer said, opening a door. The enormous room had a fireplace, too, and a huge four-poster bed made out of weathered tree trunks. "Josh's room is across the hall." She indicated a room almost the duplicate of mine. Our suitcases had appeared as if by magic.

"Why don't you two change into something more comfortable, and join us on the terrace? We'll eat out there, if it's warm enough." Jennifer went off.

Josh followed me into my room. "Something's up. Did it strike you as funny that when Tyler's name came up, nobody said a word about the Unicorn situation?"

"You didn't either, I noticed. . . . You don't suppose SMN's affected in some way by Unicorn's troubles?"

"Just don't mention that *I* am, understand? See you in a few minutes. Keep your antenna out." Josh vanished.

I wasn't quite sure what constituted casual dressing on this grand level, but I put on the raw silk slacks my mother had loaned me, and the oversized hand-knit top my grandmother'd given me for Christmas.

I stepped back into the corridor just as Josh was emerging from across the hall. He had, most uncharacteristically, brought along a pair of jeans. Jeans on Josh meant one thing only — he was anticipating a situation calling for physical activity and skullduggery. His eyes, for the first time since the Unicorn news broke, were alive with possibilities. My heart leaped. He quirked his eyebrows at me, and we went back to the living room just as Jennifer was opening the front door to let the Tylers in.

Tracy Tyler was my age, or a few years older, and she was gorgeous. She, too, was wearing pants and a big top. Her outfit was emerald green, which set off auburn hair and matched green eyes that were very, very worried.

The look in them caught my gaze and held it. Then Jeremy Tyler loomed behind her, and I'm ashamed to admit that for several minutes I was conscious of nothing, and no one, else.

The impact of his sheer *presence*, and power, was so strong, it wasn't till later that I could analyze the parts. He moved like an athlete, like a European, with an elegance that was innate, not conscious. He had dark hair, slightly wavy, and piercing, deep blue eyes. What he had on, I couldn't begin to tell you. Something about him, something I couldn't put my finger on, seemed hauntingly familiar.

It was a full five minutes before I *could* put my finger on the reason. Jeremy Tyler was everything Josh wanted to be, twenty years from now. Then it struck me like a ton of bricks that despite the maturity in his eyes, Jeremy Tyler wasn't any twenty years older than me. Maybe not even ten. I felt myself blushing, and filling with confusion.

I also felt Josh's eyes on me, with a very strange expression. When our glances met, he broke the contact quickly, turning to Tracy with a lordly air.

Equivocal was the mildest word to describe my feelings as he went out on the terrace, where Sam Kennedy was grilling crab legs over a mesquite fire.

It was more a deck or balcony, really, than a terrace. The tiled floors, and the wrought-iron railings, projected out over a slight canyon. Beyond it, the lights of other dwellings twinkled in the night. The evening was chilly, but Sam built a fire in the terrace's adobe firepit.

The crab legs were wonderful; so were the guacamole and gazpacho and the salad. I noticed those things along with noticing the vibrations going on. There was one general heading that accounted for all those vibes, and the name of that heading was Unicorn Unlimited.

Unicorn Unlimited, and the big troubles it was in. The awareness of those troubles hovered over everything, unacknowledged, like an uninvited guest.

Everyone made small talk. Sam asked how Josh and I had gotten into hacking, and I told them how I'd started fooling around with Dad's Apple as soon as he'd brought it home. Josh gave what was for him a modest account of his own computer career thus far, and his college plans.

"Were you into computers in high school?" Josh asked Sam. His tone was so deceptively mild that my ears perked up. Josh was embarking on a fishing expedition.

Sam shook his head. "In those days there were only mainframes, and child prodigies were definitely not allowed near them. I got into computing, along with Thor Jorgensen, in the service. The possibility of inventing what we now call personal computers intrigued me. Small-sized, compact, affordable. And multicompatible."

"Like Samantha," I put in.

Four pairs of eyes looked at me blankly. "That's what we call the Gemini you sent us. It suits her personality, I think," I said sweetly.

Sam let out a roar of laughter. "It does suit her. Yes, like Samantha. If she does everything she's designed to, she represents a major breakthrough."

"She does," I said. "I'll give you a demonstration, if you want, tomorrow."

Sam and Jeremy exchanged glances. "I hope you don't have the Gemini prototype around unguarded," Jeremy said involuntarily, and Sam replied, "Relax. It's here. It's safe."

Josh and I looked at each other across the glass-topped table. So Jeremy Tyler knew about Samantha's special features. And this comfortable, relaxed house was actually like a fortress; it needed to be. Partly, but not only, because of Sam's inventions like Samantha. Those facts could not have come through more clearly if the two men had shouted them out loud.

It was at this point that I became aware of a kind of pull upon me. As if somebody was trying to establish mental telepathy with me, the way I do with Samantha. And it wasn't Josh. It wasn't Jeremy. It came from Jennifer Kennedy. As I looked up, startled, she smiled at me and said clearly, "Sidney and Josh aren't just hackers, you know. They're detectives. You must have seen them on TV in the news a week or so ago. They foiled a psychotic killer who was terrorizing the cast and crew of the soap opera, *Lust for Life*, when no one else had been able to solve the problem."

I looked around the table swiftly. Jennifer seemed to be trying to tell Jeremy something. Jeremy was staring Tracy down, and Tracy looked torn and anguished. Josh —

I blinked. Josh was gazing at Tracy with the expression of an Eastern potentate contemplating an addition to his harem.

"Jeremy started out the way you two have," Jennifer said, smiling at him. "Jeremy's one of my child-prodigy computer clients. He's been programming since he was — what, twelve?"

"Ten." It was Tracy who answered, not Jeremy.

Josh hitched his chair forward. "What I've always wondered," he asked persuasively, "is with your brains, whatever made you go into writing computer games?"

Jeremy, for the first time, laughed. "I was bored to death in a required freshman statistics class they wouldn't let me out of."

Josh groaned. "I know. Sidney and I are stuck in a computer class like that."

"So to keep myself awake I fooled around with ways to make the material more interesting. My first game was *Probability*. *High Roller!* followed it."

"The good old American success story," Sam said blandly. But his eyes were alert. I realized he was prodding Jeremy to open up. I was beginning to get a suspicion of something else, as well. "Three best-selling games in a row, in a highly competitive field."

"It wasn't three in a row, and you know it," Jeremy said. "Two other games died quiet deaths, and a third never reached the market."

"*Numero Uno*," Josh said, deliberately baiting him, "is probably going to do as well as your earlier successes. The *Wall Street Journal* said so."

"It's too soon to tell," Jeremy said shortly.

Tracy turned toward me, her green eyes blazing. "Did you know my brother was in college when he was sixteen? He invented *Probability* his first year, and he formed Unicorn Unlimited only one year later. He and Brian Ellerbee and Ivan Hatch. But Jeremy's the brains behind Unicorn. Everyone knows that."

"I certainly do," Josh said, not moving.

"So do I," Sam Kennedy said firmly. He was speaking to Tracy, but it wasn't Tracy he was looking at. It was straight to Jeremy

Tyler's face that he said, "Unicorn Unlimited is Jeremy Tyler's baby. Jeremy Tyler's responsible for Unicorn's successes, but not its failures. Or for any gambling tie-in. *So isn't it about time both you Tylers stopped trying to cover up who is?*"

Chapter 5

For a minute everything was still, as though a flashbulb had gone off, freezing and capturing the scene. Then Jeremy Tyler rose.

"I've had more than enough of Unicorn Unlimited for one day. Sam, Jen, it was a wonderful dinner, as usual." Meticulously courteous, he shook hands with Josh and me. "A pleasure meeting you. I'll see you, I'm sure, at the exhibit. Come, Tracy."

Tracy followed, flashing Jennifer an anguished glance.

"I warned you," Jennifer said to Sam when they had gone.

"Well, *somebody* had to say something," Sam retorted. "You're his lawyer, but even you haven't gotten him to face reality. He's too pig-headed!"

"And you," Jennifer said evenly, "are his friend, not his attorney."

In accord, Josh and I began making noises about how tired we were after our cross-country flight.

I half expected Josh to follow me into my room, but he muttered, "Talk to you in the morning," and disappeared behind his own door, his forehead furrowed.

I had a lot to think about myself, but I didn't think long. Before I knew it, the sun was streaming in through the lacy branches of the pepper tree outside my window. And then there weren't just branches moving behind the filmy curtains, but a human shape.

I sat up, heart hammering and sleep vanishing, and Josh's voice, low-pitched, said, "It's just me."

He came in as I reached for my robe, sat down in the chair by the fireplace, and said, "Some night."

"Some night. In all senses. What did you make of it?"

"I'll tell you one thing," Josh said, looking me straight in the eyes. "You were right about it not being the time to throw in the towel on my Unicorn investment. About my giving up too soon, without a fight. And about something weird going on. Something more in *our* line."

Such a concession of fallible judgment, from Josh, was magnificent. I was very careful not to look like I was gloating.

"Okay," I said matter-of-factly. "What have you concluded?"

"Sam was right. Tyler is covering something. Or somebody."

"So's his sister."

Josh frowned. "She looked to me more like

an innocent victim. She looked terribly hurt. As if somebody's been treating her unfairly."

He had that fatuous look on his face again.

"You should know. You do *love* rescuing damsels in distress, don't you?" I couldn't believe it was my own voice saying that.

Josh stared at me. "I seem to remember there were a few times when it was a good thing for you I did."

"Meaning I couldn't have handled things without you?"

"Meaning nothing of the sort. Don't put words into my mouth. I'm simply trying to point out that I observed Miss Tyler seemed very troubled."

"You would notice. You were looking at her hard enough."

"Why wouldn't I? She's spectacular," Josh said with dignity. His eyebrow rose. "Of course, you were so busy noticing her spectacular brother."

All of a sudden we were staring each other down, and breathing hard.

"I think," I said shakily, "we'd better get back to the case."

"It's not a case, not officially. It's our private investigation. But," Josh said, carefully businesslike, "one thing I concluded, reviewing last night's conversation: The Kennedys are hoping Tyler hires us."

"I'll tell you something else," I said, just as carefully. "I can't prove it, but I'll bet you anything that's the real reason the Kennedys brought us to California. Not because of

Samantha. Not because of the computer show."

Josh's brows shot up. "But they invited us two weeks ago. Before the congressional investigation into gambling started, let alone friend Shuttleworth's crusade."

"Which means, doesn't it, that they had some kind of advance knowledge about what was going to happen?"

We stared at each other.

"I don't like having you mixed up in it."

"Just *try* and keep me out," I said dangerously.

"Of course, you do have stock in the matter, too." Josh, pleased with his pun, kissed me haphazardly on top of the head and wandered off to dress.

That Unicorn stock he'd bought for me was going to become an issue, but the time to fight that out wasn't now. I was just relieved to see him back to his old self and not thinking about that college money. Even if he *was* noticing spectacular redheads.

I studiously avoided thinking about Jeremy Tyler — and my reaction to him — as I dressed.

I was brushing my hair when a knock sounded on the door.

"It's Jennifer. Are you awake? May I come in?" She had brought me a glass of fresh-squeezed orange juice and the day's plans. "Sam's going to SMN right after breakfast. He wants to check your Samantha out while the place is empty. He'll be going to the hotel to check the SMN display sometime in the day. I have SMN entertainment errands, and then some work to do at my law office. Then there's the charity preview and SMN's buffet. You and Josh are welcome to do whatever you like till it's time for those."

She was making no reference at all to the scene last night, so I didn't, either. "We'd both like to see the SMN plant," I said politely.

"Mike's driving Sam there at eight. You can go to the plant with him then, or some time later."

"We'd like to go this morning. Thank you." I decided to do some fishing. "Does Sam always go to the plant on weekends? And who's Mike?"

"(A) Need you ask? (B) Mike's our chauffeur, go-fer, general what-would-we-do-without-him type."

"Bodyguard?"

Jennifer became alert. "What made you ask that?"

"I just wondered. From what I hear, it just seems to . . . go with the territory."

"I'm afraid it does. Anyway, Mike's a good friend of Sam's, someone Sam can unwind with, so having him around's a good idea. Are you ready for breakfast?"

I went to the dining room with her, thinking hard.

Josh was already at the table, deep in a discussion with Sam about Samantha's mind-reading capabilities. Sam kept right on talking about Samantha when we were in the Mercedes, being driven to SMN. Josh and I shared the back seat's glories this time, and Sam sat up front with his go-fer/chauffeur/bodyguard.

Mike Kubiczek was not what I'd expected. For starters, he was a whole lot younger, around Jeremy Tyler's age, and he clearly thought I was old enough for him. *And* that he was God's gift to women, though he had none of Jeremy Tyler's (or Josh's) style. He gave me a meaningful, up-and-down glance when we were introduced, and Josh looked wary. I was glad I didn't have to ride in the front seat.

Other than that, Mike was nondescript. *Surprisingly so for a bodyguard*, I thought. Then I recognized the muscles in the tanned arms under the plaid sport shirt.

The SMN plant was a big surprise. I'd heard a lot about how Sam had started out — on pennies and prayers, in an old Army quonset hut — and the image must have stuck in my mind. But SMN had grown up in the years since then. It was housed now in a sleek low building, gleaming white and California-modern. There were landscaped grounds, a swimming pool, tennis court, even a fishing stream and jogging paths.

"What's good for the worker is good for the company, and vice versa." Sam chuckled at our reaction as the Mercedes purred past these splendors and up the drive. "This has always been a we're-all-in-it-together operation, right from the first. We've been able to expand a lot since we went public."

"Like Unicorn?" Josh asked alertly.

"You could say that."

There had been no gate at the entrance to the drive, but there were guards at the main door where Mike let us out. There were electronic devices at all doors, as we moved through the building from one department to another. "There are Dobermans on patrol at night," Sam told us.

I'd heard words like *billion dollar companies, computer theft, priceless innovations* slung around a lot. Now it was beginning to register on me, in tangible terms, what those things implied.

Then Sam slipped a special coded card into a slot to open the research-and-development-area door, and all other astonishments faded from my mind. The world-of-the future products being developed in the lab dwarfed my imagination. Josh, unlike me, understood computer innards. He and Sam assembled Samantha, carrying on an almost foreign-language discussion of her operating system all the while, and Sam installed the new no-booting-up-needed chip and showed us how it worked.

"I'd like to see an alpha-state demonstration," he said, when Samantha was back in one piece and winking coquettishly.

"Mental telepathy's Sidney's department," Josh said.

I don't know how to describe alpha state

very well. It's an altered state of consciousness, a kind of trance. It feels like being on a
kind of automatic pilot. I've always fallen
into alpha easily when I daydream, and I've
learned how to put myself into it on cue, even
in pretty hairy situations. I always feel pretty
silly going through this in front of anybody,
even Josh. But I have to admit it was satisfying to show off now.

I fed Samantha the special program I'd
devised, and settled eyeball-to-eyeball with
her red-and-green blinking lights. *Concen-
trate and focus. . . . Send the thought-message:*

*Samantha . . . Samantha. . . . Are you with
me?*

DON'T ASK SILLY QUESTIONS.
OF COURSE I'M WITH YOU, Samantha
blinked back at me with annoyance.

Vaguely, somewhere behind me, I heard
Sam chuckle. He was the creator of
Samantha's exasperating personality, of
course. I resolutely tuned him out.

*Samantha, I'm sorry. I meant do you read
me?*

APOLOGY ACCEPTED, Samantha
answered, mollified.

Okay, if she was in that mood, she was
asking for it. And so was Sam.

Samantha, please ring the fire alarm.

DOES NOT COMPUTE, Samantha retorted smugly.

I'd asked for that, forgetting Josh hadn't
played with the electric wiring as required
for that particular stunt.

All right then, will you — I started. And stopped. Samantha was raising hell. Her screen blanked out the earlier messages. Her red and green lights went crazy. And then *Samantha* was transmitting mental telepathy to *me*, a message flashing on a kind of screen behind my eyes.

STRANGER APPROACHING. POTENTIAL DANGER!

Chapter 6

"Somebody's coming," I blurted. I sensed, rather than saw, the others tense. Sam's right hand went to his pocket — and came out with a gun. His left hand swept on a switch that activated a closed-circuit TV monitor above the door.

It showed Jennifer just outside the door, her hand raised to knock. The intercom cleared its throat and bleeped.

"Sam, are you in there? I forgot to bring my key card," Jennifer's voice said.

The scenario dissolved into comedy.

"Just because you haven't been formally introduced yet, you needn't go reading everyone as an enemy," I grumbled to Samantha, who flounced her lights at me. Josh sat back as if taking credit for the whole exchange, and Sam laughed and went to open the door for Jennifer.

"Do you people know it's nearly one o'clock? I'm stealing Josh and Sidney for lunch. Sam, Jeremy called. He tried to reach you here but got the answering service. He wants to buy you lunch at the exhibit center."

"To apologize for walking out last night, or to punch me out?" Sam inquired.

"I didn't ask. Either would be appropriate." Jennifer's lips twitched slightly. "Sam, listen. As you so graciously pointed out last night, I'm the one who's Jeremy's lawyer, not you. So please, don't start giving him any more advice! It will only make him more determined not to take any! Just try to keep his mind off Unicorn today. I'll handle the rest."

"*Are* you handling it?"

"I'm taking steps. The Mercedes is out front and Mike's waiting in your office to drive you over," Jennifer said grandly, and swept us out the back way.

When we reached her trim sports car, Josh lit up, and I understood what Jennifer meant by "taking steps"— understood, and didn't like my personal reaction. Tracy Tyler was in the back seat.

"Sidney, get in back. Josh, ride up front with me," Jennifer said crisply. I wondered, embarrassed, if she'd seen my green-eyed monster. Then I got in, and realized with shame that Jennifer had had other, more important reasons. Tracy looked terrified, and she'd been crying. She might look spectacular, she might have Josh's head spinning, but she was also vulnerable and in need of help. And Josh, with his arrogance and ego and high-handed manner, clearly intimidated her.

I closed the back door, smiled, and said lightly, "Hi. I'm glad to get a chance to see you again."

"I'm sorry about that scene last night," Tracy said in a low voice. Her hands clenched, and she threw Jennifer an imploring glance.

"I kidnapped her," Jennifer said flatly. "Sam was right last night. My genius client is acting as if he's either a first-class fool or riddled with guilt —"

Tracy's head came up swiftly. "He's not!"

"Then he'd better stop acting like it before he testifies in Washington," Jennifer snapped. "And he'd better stop trying to tie my hands. I can't protect Unicorn if he won't give me ammunition, or authorize me to get it!"

"I don't know what you're talking about," Tracy said in a small voice."

"Oh, yes, you do," a voice said bluntly, and it wasn't Jennifer's. It was Josh. He didn't turn around, he simply stated, "She's talking about SSW Enterprises, Computer Consultants. And finding out who's trying to make a profit off of the gambling scandal, *and* Unicorn, *and* your brother. And what Aldous P. Shuttleworth has up his sleeve, *before* he springs his evidence in Washington. Or on TV!"

Tracy shut her eyes, I willed Josh to shut

up, and Jennifer went on as if he hadn't spoken.

"Tracy has a stake in Unicorn. Her college money's in it. I'm not getting through to Jeremy; maybe you can get through to her. We're going to have lunch at someplace quiet, where none of the computer crowd will hear us, so you can have a talk. She's sitting on something, and she knows it."

We rode in silence for twenty minutes while I mulled this over. Josh remained discreetly silent, and Tracy sat as though carved in stone.

Jennifer pulled up at last before a charming greenhousey resturant that was all tiles and hanging plants and secluded corners. We ordered.

There was a long silence. At last Tracy lifted her green eyes, first to me, then Josh.

"How much do you know about what's going on in Unicorn?" she asked abruptly.

"Plenty. I just sank my college money in Unicorn stock, too," Josh said calmly. Tracy flinched, recovered, and turned to me.

"I know about the stock taking a nose dive since the gambling charges," I said. "I know there's something fishy about the whole situation. I know your brother started the company when he was in college, and it's had two successful games. Three, if you count *Numero Uno*. I didn't know before last night about the games that flopped, or about how Unicorn got started up in business."

Tracy took a deep breath. "Jeremy and Ivan Hatch met in college. You'll meet them at the exhibition. Ivan's a wheeler-dealer salesman. He sold Jeremy on the idea of manufacturing that first game he invented. The upshot was Jeremy founded Unicorn, and took Ivan and Brian Ellerbee in as junior partners."

"Who's this Ellerbee?" Josh asked.

"Another college friend. The kind," Tracy said carefully, "who's born middle-aged with the *Wall Street Journal* in one hand and a checkbook in the other." I stifled a grin. "Brian's a financial genius, Jeremy says."

"Where did the money to start Unicorn come from?" Josh asked bluntly.

"From what Dad left us." Tracy's eyes darkened. "Our parents were killed in a car accident. Jeremy was seventeen. He really raised me. Which was quite an accomplishment, when you consider Jeremy was doing free-lance programming and taking a double college load at the same time."

"You don't have to sell us on how great he is." Josh looked at Tracy with more sympathy than was actually called for. "It sounds as if at least he didn't have money worries."

Tracy shook her head. "There was insurance, and some other things. And Jeremy had a full college scholarship. . . . Jeremy and I put our inheritance into starting Unicorn. He didn't want to take my money, too, but I made him. Ivan and Brian Ellerbee put in their savings, too. That's how they were **able to** start manufacturing *Probability* — in a couple of rooms they sublet in Mr. Kennedy's SMN factory."

I knew the next part of the story. "*Probability* took off. And then the next year Jeremy followed it up with *High Roller!* Then they started selling Unicorn stock to outside investors, too, so they could expand production. That's when Jeremy and Hatch and Ellerbee became millionaires on paper."

And Tracy, too, I thought. She'd put her inheritance into Unicorn, too.

"Wait a minute," Josh said, frowning. "You people can't be millionaires on paper only. You must have gotten some cash when you started selling stock." Tracy nodded. "And you'd get back *at least* what you'd first put in if you sold the rest of your share right now, in spite of what's happened lately."

"But I wouldn't sell," Tracy said promptly. Josh ignored that.

"You'll make even more money if you hang on now, and sell out later after all this blows over. That may be important." He studied Tracy attentively. "What happened next?"

"Everything started changing," she said flatly. "You know. Big building, lots of employees. More and more success. Jeremy didn't pay much attention. He was all wrapped up in brainstorming new games. All brainteasers. And all of them shot down by his partners. The games were too intellectual, they said."

I could guess how that had gone over with Jeremy. "Where did the flop games come in?" I asked.

"Hatch thought Unicorn should have an arcade-type game. It bombed. I don't know why."

"And the other game that didn't work?" Josh asked.

Tracy made an involuntary movement. "Tell them," Jennifer said inexorably. "Otherwise I will."

I could feel waves of panic wash over Tracy, and apparently Josh could, too. Josh put his hand over hers and told her to take it slow and easy.

"Jeremy wanted to do a text-adventure game," Tracy said carefully. "You know, one of those multiple-choice story things. I helped him make up the story line for it, and I even worked on some of the programming."

She stopped abruptly.

"And?" I asked gently.

"And last summer, two weeks before nationwide publicity for the game was to start," Jennifer said, "a game almost exactly like it was brought out by another software company — with a big, big splash. You tell me if that isn't too much coincidence!"

"What company?" Josh asked practically. Jennifer supplied the names of both company and game, and I gasped. Both were exceedingly familiar.

"Couldn't Unicorn do anything about copyright infringement?" I demanded. Jennifer shook her head.

"Unicorn's game hadn't come out yet, and anyway, copyrights for software are still a very fuzzy issue. Jeremy refused to even report the possibility of a theft to the police. He canceled production of the Unicorn game and wrote *Numero Uno* himself — in one marathon weekend — to replace it. But he couldn't get it manufactured fast enough for last year's Christmas sales."

I was thinking hard. "If *Numero Uno* was dreamed up so fast, that could explain how the gambling implications got past Jeremy —"

"Jeremy's mind doesn't operate that way," Tracy said vehemently. "Or could the gambling features have been added to the game *after* manufacture? I don't know. I'm not a computer expert."

"You've done some programming and game development," Josh reminded her.

"Not anymore! Somehow, I must have copied the game I thought I was inventing from that other game. I don't know how! But I won't risk it happening again!"

"It doesn't make sense," I said slowly. "How could you have copied from that other game if it wasn't on the market yet?"

"*I* don't know. Maybe I heard something somewhere, or played some version that was being tested."

"There's another explanation that makes a lot more sense," Josh said flatly. "Piracy.

Somebody stole *Unicorn's* game, not the other way around. It's too bad your brother didn't go to the police right away."

"They couldn't have done anything. Piracy's too difficult to prove, and you heard what Jennifer said about copyrights." Tracy stopped. When Josh just gave her one of those "I'm waiting" looks, she added reluctantly, "At the time, Jer thought he knew who might have leaked the game. He didn't have evidence on which to prosecute, so he got rid of the person. Then he found out afterwards the person he suspected could not have done it. Anyway . . . none of that matters now."

Tracy leaned forward tensely, her eyes bright with tears. "What matters is Unicorn, and what's happening to *Numero Uno*. And to Jeremy. Somebody's trying to destroy my company. I can't prove it, and Jeremy isn't even trying to. But you two could. Jennifer's right. You're the experts. Jeremy should be hiring you, but he's too stubborn."

Tracy took a breath. "Jeremy will be furious, but I don't care anymore. I'm part owner of Unicorn, too. I want to hire SSW Enterprises Computer Consultants to clear Jeremy of these gambling charges and find out what's really going on."

"And who stole the game last summer," I said automatically. "I'd bet you anything they're related."

"*No!*" Tracy was on her feet, and she was shaking, but her voice was very firm. "I want you to investigate, but with two conditions. One, you let the business of that other game alone. It has nothing at all to do with what's going on now — innocent people could get hurt if you drag it up. Two, you do your investigating without letting my brother find out I've hired you!"

Chapter 7

"I don't like it," Josh said.

"Like what?"

"Spying on Tyler's company behind his back. And with our hands tied about what we can investigate, and what we can't."

"Would you like it better if you lost your college money and Unicorn went down the tube?" I inquired.

It was late Saturday afternoon and we were back at the house, dressing for the SMN reception. At least that's what we were supposed to be doing. Actually, we were in my room having a fight.

"It isn't ethical," Josh said stubbornly. "If Tyler wanted us to investigate him, he'd ask us."

"No, he wouldn't. He's too stubborn and proud, just like you are." I ducked into the bathroom to change my dress, leaving the door open a crack so Josh could hear me. "Or maybe he's covering something up. I don't like thinking that any more than you do. But look at the facts!"

"What facts? An anonymous police tip-off and a bunch of crackpots spreading rumors!"

"I'm not talking about that! I mean the stolen game." I zipped up my rose chiffon dress and came back out. "Nobody outside the company knows the game was stolen. Why? Nobody knows who ripped the game off. Why? And why wasn't the theft reported to the police?

"Probably because it wouldn't have been good for the company's image," Josh said. "Speaking of images, you'd better brush your hair. It's falling down."

I looked in the mirror, yanked out the barrette, and began brushing furiously. Then I twisted my hair up, secured it with Mother's art nouveau hairpin, and surveyed myself with exasperation. The dress was pretty. *I* looked pretty. And *young*. Going to an important computer show, I wanted to look like an executive: beautiful, but cosmopolitan and brainy. And decidedly not fluffy.

At that moment, I'd have settled for looking like Tracy Tyler. Josh wasn't looking at me the way he'd looked at her. He wasn't even looking at me. He was gazing out the window, frowning. "I'd feel better if Tyler would hire us himself," he said firmly. "I know you can't see it, but it's a question of ethics —"

I saw red. "Don't lecture me about business ethics. SSW Enterprises is *my* company, and Tracy wants to hire it because she needs help.

If you'd rather ogle her than do something practical, that's your problem. But don't tell me what I can or cannot do!"

Josh stalked out without a word.

The climate was pretty frigid on the way to the computer show preview. Mike drove us all in the Mercedes, and though Josh and I were squeezed tightly together in the back, we didn't exchange any remarks at all. Josh had pulled out all the stops: pin-striped navy blue suit; thin gold watch; gold cuff links; very, very conservative shirt and tie. He could have been the chairman of the board of a big corporation, and all his walls were up.

The exhibition was being held at a hotel that was almost a small world in itself. Conference wings, private entertaining wings, pools and tennis and racquetball — the works. The parking lot was jammed, and as we swept toward the hotel entrance I was startled to see a crowd of people and some TV work crews.

"Ribbon-cutting ceremony," Sam said. "With Jeremy Tyler officiating. He's the current president of our trade association."

We got out of the car, and Mike drove off. Some dignitaries joined Jeremy Tyler for the ribbon cutting. Floodlights went on, TV cameras started whirring, and the crowd of distinguished guests pressed close. That's when it happened.

From behind us, there were shrill, raucous noises. Suddenly, a demonstration was breaking out — or breaking in. The Advocates for

Children had arrived, led by Aldous P. Shuttleworth in person.

They were there to call to the attention of the world the vicious exploitation of America's innocent youth by Jeremy Tyler and his infamous Unicorn Unlimited. Complete with placards and sandwich boards, they pushed through till they were nose-to-nose with Jeremy.

It was happening so fast that nobody knew what to do, except the TV people, who ate it up. Aldous P. Shuttleworth was brandishing a portable computer, on which he intended to demonstrate — for the cameras — the evil gambling usages of *Numero Uno*. Then the guards, galvanized, hustled the demonstrators to one side. A few people got roughed up. I heard somebody shouting about the Bill of Rights, and the hotel manager saying with great control that they could demonstrate in the parking lot, but not in front of the door.

Instinctively, I looked around for Josh, but could not find him. Sam, too, had vanished. At last, order was restored. Reporters still clamored, thrusting microphones into Jeremy's face. "Do you wish to respond to the charges, Mr. Tyler?" "There are rumors Unicorn is close to bankruptcy. Would you care to comment?"

Jennifer pushed her way through to shield Jeremy. "Unicorn Unlimited has no comment at the present time," she said as microphones swung toward her.

"Are you a spokesman for the company?"

"Jennifer Kennedy, Mr. Tyler's attorney. I *can* tell you there's no truth to the bankruptcy rumors." Jennifer smiled, a wry, amused smile that lowered the tension several levels. "If we ever get this charity preview opened, Unicorn Unlimited will show you several exciting new software products. And give you a chance to play *Numero Uno*, if you want to check its 'harmful effects' out for yourselves!"

Somebody tried to insert a question about the congressional hearing. Jennifer cut him off. "Unicorn Unlimited will be issuing a statement later. Thank you, ladies and gentlemen. That will be all for now."

For heaven's sake, cut the ribbon! I willed the words toward Jeremy Tyler. He cut it. The doors swung open; the invited guests swarmed inside. The demonstrators were held firmly back by police that had belatedly appeared.

I was swept inside on the glamorously-dressed tide. No one that I knew was near me. This wasn't just a charity preview, or a trade show. It was a media event, to which Unicorn's troubles added extra excitement.

I started introducing myself as "President of SSW Enterprises," and handing out business cards, like all the others did. I visited the SMN booth and was introduced to two of Sam's biggest clients. When I came upon the Unicorn booth, Jeremy Tyler saw me approaching and gave me a megavolt smile.

I could feel my knees turning to jelly and

my face growing pink. I had to summon all my poise as Jeremy introduced me to his two partners.

"Brian Ellerbee, financial vice-president of Unicorn. Ivan Hatch, vice-president, sales. Sidney Scott Webster, president of SSW Enterprises. It's a programming and data-crunching firm."

We murmured to each other as I eyed them. If Jeremy Tyler was what Josh could be fifteen years from now, Brian Ellerbee was what he'd turn into if he wasn't careful: the same black hair, the same pin-striped suit, the same tendency to be very buttoned-up-tight. Ellerbee made me think of a machine, with a computer program instead of a brain — or a heart. As for Ivan Hatch, I could picture him on the tennis court, or jogging trail. I could picture him selling, too. He looked like a model in a magazine ad, and a little too picture-perfect. A little too much the kind of person who was always out for Number One. And I didn't mean the game, *Numero Uno*.

I told them both how glad I was to meet them, and asked Jeremy if his sister was around.

"Somewhere or other. She's giving Josh the grand tour, I believe," Jeremy said.

Hmmmm.

I thanked him politely and moved on with what I hoped was a queenly air.

I was beginning to get a handle on how to "work the crowd," as Josh would no doubt put it. *I* wasn't working it for jobs, like others were, but the principle was the same. Be polite, be friendly, be genuinely interested. Keep moving. Keep the computer in the brain recording what you say, and see, and hear.

What I didn't see or hear anywhere was Josh and Tracy, but I was picking up a good bit else. The congressional investigation of computer games was a hot topic. And the possible tie-in between Unicorn and organized gambling was the hottest rumor. By the time I'd circulated for an hour, my blood was boiling.

The exhibition occupied the main floor and balcony of the grand ballroom. In the center of the floor was a kind of raised dais that was the focus of a lot of flashing lights. I headed for it. TV cameras were whirring as some vaguely familiar figures posed beside one of the world's biggest computer companies' baby. I was edging in for a closer look when a man's voice, surprised and pleased and totally unexpected, said, "Sidney Webster, for heaven's sake!"

I looked up, startled. My Aunt Jane's boyfriend, the actor Ross Taylor from her soap opera, *Lust for Life*, was leaning down toward me from the dais.

"What are *you* doing here?" I asked, astonished.

"Promotion, what else? We're adding a Silicon Valley story line to *Lust*. So four of us are here on location for a few days — without Jane, unfortunately — and the sponsor's sent us here today for free publicity. The company my soap character owns is buying out a high tech firm. Good chance for skullduggery." Ross grinned.

I didn't, and he saw it. His face changed. "You didn't come all the way to California to look at new computer products, did you? What *are* you doing here? Another criminal investigation?"

Somewhere near us, somebody went tense. I felt it, rather than saw it, and when I whirled around there was nothing *to* see. Everything was normal.

But that reaction had been there, all the same.

Chapter 8

All this lasted for only a minute. Then Ross said, "Sidney?" and one of the cameramen who'd been aiming at Ross caught sight of Jeremy Tyler, and recognized him. I acted on instinct.

I interposed myself in front of the camera as Jennifer had done, gave the crew my most brilliant smile, and said clearly, "I'm Sidney Scott Webster, SSW Enterprises, Lakeland, New Jersey." From the corner of my eye I saw that Jeremy Tyler had performed a vanishing act. I was shaking in my shoes, but I hoped it didn't show. "Ross Taylor and I know each other from his show, *Lust for Life*."

"Have you appeared on the show?" A reporter thrust a microphone toward me.

"Miss Webster's a star at the computer," Ross said. "She's been of enormous help to *Lust for Life*. She was the person last month who —"

"Hey, I remember," the cameraman interrupted, looking at me sharply. "Weren't you the one who caught that weirdo —"

"My company did the research on storyline preferences among viewers nationwide," I said loudly, wishing I dared risk shooting a look to Ross. Acclaim as computer detectives was all very well, but at this moment it might not be an advantage.

The reporter said quickly, looking at me hard, "Would your being here have anything to do with the accusations being made against Unicorn Industries?"

My heart lurched. It was the network reporter who'd been giving Jeremy the hard time earlier. Clearly she'd remembered the publicity about Josh and me being "computer detectives," and had made the obvious connection.

I wanted to get away from there without appearing evasive, or arousing suspicion in any quarters. I wanted to check out who had been responsible for that sudden tension when Ross had spoken to me. It would not be easy. "I've played Unicorn games a couple of times," I said lightly. "Hasn't everybody?"

I started to ease myself away and heard, "Sidney! I've been looking for you! Unicorn Unlimited wants to talk business with us."

Josh, with his normal lord-of-the-manor tone, as if our earlier frigid silences had never been. Josh, bearing down on me with Brian Ellerbee and Ivan Hatch behind him.

The air crackled. People's ears started flapping. Cameras and microphones swung toward us. Josh ignored them. He could have been in a private office, I thought irately, for all he cared about people listening in. "I've been discussing SSW's work with these gentlemen," Josh went on blandly, "and they're interested in discussing terms for SSW to create a videogame for Unicorn's Christmas sales."

"Game programming isn't part of SSW's services," I said frigidly.

"Don't be modest!" Ivan Hatch flashed a charming smile, half to me, half to the TV cameras. "Rivington's been telling us the sensational game idea you've been developing. We certainly want to kick the ball around with you before you offer it to anyone else."

"But I haven't —"

The heel of Josh's boot came down, hard, on my toe.

"She hasn't any intention of revealing her idea till you make her an offer in writing. Isn't that right, Miss Webster? After all, game ideas are gold, and nobody reveals the strike till the claim's been filed. Ha ha." Josh was being his most obnoxious. "Mr. Ellerbee, the next move's up to you."

"Brian Ellerbee? Vice-President of Unicorn Unlimited?" The mike swung in front of Ellerbee so fast it made a breeze. "Will you comment on Unicorn Unlimited's current troubles and on these young people's involvement with them?"

"I'd be happy to comment." Ivan Hatch planted himself between Josh and me, his hands resting on our shoulders. "Unicorn Unlimited is signing up these fine young people to create a totally new type of computer game. I'm not at liberty to tell you much about it. But it will be highly educational, stimulate children's creativity, and be good clean fun. You already know, I'm sure, of the fine backgrounds of these youngsters here. . . ."

He went on and on. I felt like being sick. It was a wonder Josh didn't, too. But no, there he stood, with a copy of Ellerbee's tight smile. Fortunately the reporter soon had enough of this, also. Unfortunately, she turned the microphone in my direction.

"All I can tell you is that we're negotiating," I said with my best Mona Lisa smile. And then, blessedly, Ross Taylor intervened. He reached out for Josh's hand, and shook it, and introduced himself to the Unicorn boys. Ivan Hatch, scenting publicity possibilities in a TV actor, latched onto Ross. The reporters hounded off in search of other targets.

Brian Ellerbee buttonholed me. "When can we talk?"

"I'll let you know."

"Breakfast tomorrow? It would be splendid if we could release the news about the game during this exhibition."

Haven't you hogged the cameras enough already? I thought viciously. "I'll let you know, after my associate and I confer," I said firmly.

* * *

Josh got the message. "See you again while you're here, I hope," he said to Ross, and slipping my arm through his, led me off as if we were on a date.

"Mr. Rivington," I said dangerously, "we have to talk."

"I know it. We're going to." Josh marched me straight out the entryway of the exhibition hall.

"Joshua Rivington, what do you think you're doing —"

"Just keep quiet and come on." Josh steered me out the door and down the winding steps to a terrace beside the swimming pool. Nobody was swimming at this hour, but the area was lit with elaborate lighting concealed in shrubs and trees. Josh stopped at an umbrella table and set his attache case on it.

"Nobody should be able to hear us here."

"What are you cooking up?" I demanded suspiciously.

"Unicorn games. You heard Ellerbee. He's gone bats over the idea of you doing a game for them."

"*You're* bats if you think I'll do it. And what was the idea of telling those men I have a game already under wraps?"

"To hook them, that's what," Josh said calmly. "Don't you see? You *do* want to investigate Unicorn, don't you? Here's a way to get us into the company officially without having to sneak around. So it would all be ethical. They need a new game after the mess

Numero Uno's gotten into, and they'll pay us plenty. You should be able to bang a game out easily."

"How would you know? You've never tried it," I said acidly. "You were pretty high and mighty superior about computer games till you started getting hooked on *Numero Uno.* Not to mention hero-worshipping Jeremy Tyler!"

"That has nothing to do with it," Josh said, reddening.

"The heck it doesn't!" I stopped myself in time from saying I supposed Tracy's green eyes hadn't anything to do with the whole thing, either. "You seemed to forget I already *have* a job. Finding out what's behind the attacks on Unicorn is more important than making games up for it."

"Not to the Unicorn executives, apparently," Josh said smugly.

"*Hatch and Ellerbee?* They could care less whether I created something salable or not. You heard them! 'Fine young people' . . . 'fine backgrounds of these *youngsters!*'" I mimicked savagely. "They want to trade on us being young and squeaky-clean, to combat the bad press Unicorn's been getting. Hatch sees publicity in us, and Ellerbee sees dollar signs, and what it boils down to is they're trying to exploit us."

"Good grief," Josh exploded. "Do you think Ellerbee's speech didn't make me want to gag? But there's no law that says we can't give them a dose of their own medicine, is there? *We* can take advantage of *them*. SSW gets good publicity — and maybe good royalties — if the game catches on. At any rate, we can ask for a good advance up front. They need us bad enough that they'll give it to us. And in the meantime, we'll be on the inside of their operation."

His argument was irrefutable. There was just one problem: No way in the world did I want to have anything to do with Hatch and Ellerbee. They made me feel uneasy. While I was fishing for a businesslike way to say it, Josh came in with what he clearly thought was his clincher.

"We'll be working for Unicorn, and Jeremy Tyler will know it. So there won't be a question of ethics anymore. And you won't have to tackle the Unicorn investigation without my help."

"Oh, won't I?" I looked at Josh being his most patronizing, and my wrath boiled over. "You know the trouble with you, Mr. Joshua J. Rivington III? You're trying to have your cake and eat it, too! You didn't want to run the risk of finding out your computer-genius idol might have feet of clay, and you also didn't want to miss the chance to play Sir Lancelot to a damsel in distress! Do you honestly think it's any more *ethical* to *snoop around* Jeremy Tyler's company when you're working under a contract he'd signed? Or were you counting on the fact that his signing it would mean you'd have to keep quiet about any evidence that would point to *him*?

Just how open-minded did you intend to be?"

Josh just looked at me. "About as open-minded as you could be, considering the size of the crush you've got upon the man."

"I'll pretend I didn't hear that," I said carefully, when I could speak. "I'll leave you to think of an excuse you can give to Hatch & Ellerbee & Company, about why I'm not going to do their precious game."

I stalked off, feeling as though I might be sick.

Chapter 9

Back in the grand ballroom, the wheeling and the dealing rumbled on while I stood motionless and shivered inside. Presently Jennifer saw me and came over. "Come along and have some buffet," she said, linking her arm through mine.

SMN had reserved a banquet room for a sumptuous feast. There were shrimp and clams and oysters in their shells, heaped on ice around a huge ice sculpture. There were crab legs and claws with horseradish and mustard sauces. There were Mexican and Vietnamese and Californian specialties. And there was a lot of liquor flowing, which made me feel uncomfortable.

Jennifer had left, and Sam was swallowed up by customers. I fixed myself a plate and sat down in one corner of an enormous, overstuffed off-white sofa, feeling like Alice-through-the-looking-glass.

"You don't look as if you're having much of a good time," a voice said, familiarly, close at hand.

I turned, startled. Mike Kubiczek had come up behind me. He'd dressed up for the occasion in a sports jacket and slacks, and he wore a gold chain with his open-necked shirt. He sat down on the sofa arm and nodded toward the high-powered groups around us. "How come you're not circulating and pressing the flesh? I thought this kind of thing would be right up your alley."

I blinked, and to my dismay he slid an arm around me and gave me a little squeeze. *"Come on!* I know your racket. Sam hasn't been exactly silent, you know, about the hot-shot baby geniuses."

Mike wasn't trying to make a pass at me. Or was he? His arm was still around my shoulders, and his fingers rested on my bare arm. I moved away slightly.

Mike leaned around to scan my face. "Are you here on a case? Sam's not having any problems he's not telling me about, is he? Or are you two here on account of his dear old buddy Tyler?"

"Josh and I are here on vacation. And to see the computer show," I answered primly. And then it occurred to me that here could be a valuable source of information, almost in my lap, so to speak.

I glanced up at him sideways and then down. "What made you think of Jeremy Tyler?" I asked casually.

"Unicorn Unlimited's going to go under. Everybody in the business knows it," Mike said scornfully. "I thought maybe Sam

brought you two here on the sly to pull
Tyler's chestnuts out of the fire."

"I'm definitely not working for either one
of them."

"So this is just a social visit? And you're
bored to death by this whole shindig, aren't
you?" Mike's fingers traced their way lightly
down my arm. "The boss won't be ready to
leave for an hour or more. Why don't we cut
out and find something more interesting?"

"The lady doesn't need any help from you,"
a voice said coldly.

It was Josh's voice. Josh was standing
there with his glass of Perrier, looking as
though he'd like to throw it in Mike's face. He
gave Mike his absolutely most offensive stare,
and Mike said, "Excuse *me*," elaborately, and
took off. I glared at Josh, and Josh glared
right back.

"Don't you have any more sense than to
mess around with a creep like that?"

"He's a friend of Sam's. He also talks a lot,
and if it's any of your business — which it's
not — I was just starting to pump him for
some leads. And I do not need a chaperone,
thank you very much."

"What you need is a bodyguard," Josh said
flatly.

"I can take care of myself."

"*That* I very much doubt."

"You declined to have anything to do with
this case, so kindly keep out of the way and
let me get on with it." I was starting to
breathe hard and talk very fast, which made

77

me madder. "Just remember, Mr. Rivington III, you don't *own* me."

"That," Josh said coldly, "you have made abundantly clear." He turned on his boot heel and strode off, leaving me light-headed, with my pulses pounding, and more than a little scared.

I didn't want to run the risk of Mike swarming his way back. I'd be better off in the grand ballroom, among the exhibit crowds. At least there, I hoped, there'd be Jennifer or the Tylers or Ross with whom I could take refuge.

A group of SMN customers was about to leave, so I slipped out with them and rode down in their elevator. There were still a lot of people in the grand ballroom, but I could not find Jennifer. I spotted Ross off to one side, helping the *Lust for Life* crowd wind up their duties. I was starting toward them when someone ran up and clutched my arm.

"Sidney! Oh, thank goodness." It was Tracy, her eyes enormous. "Have you seen my brother?"

"No, I just —"

"Then will you come with me, please?" She pulled me over to one side and spoke rapidly in a very low voice. "I got a call at the Unicorn display just now —"

"Man or woman?" I asked automatically.

"Man, I think. I don't know! Will you just listen? He said to tell Mr. Tyler that if he'd go to the Unicorn plant at ten P.M., he'd find evidence of what was behind Unicorn's troubles. He hung up before I could ask anything."

"Could you recognize —" I started to say. Tracy shook her head.

"It sounded disguised. Sidney, please! I can't find Jeremy anywhere, or Jennifer. I want to get there before ten, in case there's . . . anything to see when the evidence is delivered. Only I don't want to go alone."

"I'll come. I'll get Josh —"

"There isn't time! Not unless you see him right away. Ellerbee was in the booth when the call came, and I'm afraid he overheard. He disappeared while I was looking for Jeremy, and I don't trust — if he gets there first — Sidney, just *come*! I'll get my car and meet you at the front door!"

She dashed off as I thought frantically, then rushed for Ross, thanking my stars that he was now alone.

"Find Josh. And Jeremy Tyler, if you can. Make them go to the Unicorn plant as fast as possible. Something's going to happen there. I'm leaving now, with Tracy Tyler."

I ran out.

Tracy was out front with a small Volkswagen. I don't know what her driving was like normally, but she drove then as if she were in a TV car chase. I buckled my seat belt, hung on, and prayed hard.

How far away the Unicorn plant was, I don't know, but it seemed miles. We hurtled down the freeway and into a hidden drive. The Unicorn plant, all in darkness, loomed like a monolith.

"No one's here," I said aloud. And then a voice whispered in my head, *Or is there?* It was still . . . too deserted.

"I want to get where I can see." Tracy parked behind some shrubbery and opened her door. "I'm going to get behind those bushes by the front entrance. You watch from here. See if you can see a license plate."

She stepped out, a slight figure silvered by faint moonlight.

There was no sound, not even birds, nor insects humming. Everything was preternaturally still. *It looks like a scene from a movie,* that little voice said. *Or a soap opera.*

In a soap opera, this would be a trap.

The hairs on the back of my neck began to rise.

"Tracy, come back!" I called. And then, as she didn't stop, I opened my own door and jumped out. I ran toward her, reaching her just a few steps from the too-thick shrubbery that could so easily be concealing a crouching figure.

I reached her, grabbed her, jerked her back and away. And then, just as I flung her past me towards the car, I heard a great crack as though the sky had split. The heavens turned red, and I went down into fire and darkness.

Chapter 10

It was dark and cold, and I was floundering.
I tried to struggle up through that dark sea
to consciousness and light, but hands held me
back. I fought, and then I heard a voice. It
was Josh's voice. Josh, hoarse and shouting.
Josh, sounding terrified and angry. "*Sidney!*
Sidney, can you hear me? Are you all right?"

He almost never called me Sidney. It was
always Webster. I opened my eyes with
effort, and Josh's face was only an inch or
two from mine. I'd never seen it look like that,
not even on other occasions when I'd almost
gotten killed. "Sidney. . . thank God. I
thought I'd gotten here too late —" His voice
was cracking.

"I'll live," I said through dry lips. "What
hap —" Then I remembered. "Tracy!
Where's Tracy?"

Josh's face went absolutely blank. That's
something I'll always remember; it went
absolutely blank and his voice, ashamed and
sheepish, said, "I don't know. I didn't
think —"

He hadn't thought of Tracy. He'd only thought of me. I hugged the meaning of it to my heart even as I said, anxiously, "She was with me. I pushed her off, away from — I have to find —"

"No!" Josh said sharply, holding my shoulders down. "I'll find out." He glanced behind him, swiftly, then turned back. "She's in one piece. She's sitting up; Ross has her. So she can't be hurt, at least not very much. Webster, *no*! Let Ross take care of her. Don't try to move until an ambulance gets here."

"If you think I'm going to lie here like a corpse," I muttered grimly, "think again."

"You shouldn't move if you have broken bones."

"So find out." My head ached horribly, but I didn't think anything else was wrong. Josh touched me all over, carefully, and he hit sore spots, but nothing bad enough to make me cry aloud. "You'll live," he said at last. "I guess." His face came down on mine.

"Why, Mr. Rivington," I whispered shakily, "whatever will people think?"

"So call it mouth-to-mouth resuscitation," Josh said, and started kissing me again.

We were interrupted by Ross looming over us. "Tracy's sitting up by her car. She's bruised, that's all. I'll have to leave you here and go for help. I saw a gas —"

A siren shrieked.

It was echoed by another, coming closer. And then spinning red lights — like Samantha's, only magnified — were rivaling the red glow in the sky . . . a flickering glow. I turned my head and saw flames licking against Unicorn's front entryway.

"Don't look," Josh said, trying to hold me still.

"The heck I won't," I retorted firmly. "Tell me what happened."

"I got your message. We couldn't find Jeremy, so we left word with Sam and took off after you." Josh talked fast, for an ambulance crew and firemen were tumbling toward us. "We drove in — I saw you by the entrance — Then the bomb went off. I was sure you'd been killed —"

"Okay, buddy, we'll take over now." Two paramedics knelt beside me, pulling Josh away. They had a stretcher waiting, and wouldn't listen when I said I was all right. "You're going to the emergency room, both you girls. Don't you give us a hard time, too," the younger paramedic said pleasantly.

So I gave in, because I wanted Tracy to go and wanted to be with her. "I'm coming, too," Josh said firmly, and I yelled, "No! Please! Check things out!"

Josh was torn, but he agreed. The last thing I saw as I was being booted into the ambulance was Josh striding toward Jeremy's car as it careened in, brakes screaming, silhouetted against a sullen sky.

This was not the first time I'd been in a hospital emergency room. Suffice to say one E.R.'s like another, and they gave me a hard time because I was under age and had no parent handy. At last they agreed to let me go, provided someone came to claim me. By that time Tracy, too, was putting up a fight to leave, and then Jeremy arrived, with Josh in tow.

We were exiting by one door just as police put in an appearance at another. "Come on!" Josh said curtly, and grabbing me (gingerly), hustled me toward Jeremy's car. Jeremy, picking up the cue, did the same with Tracy. We tumbled into a car that, even in that state, I realized was quite something, and took off at a rate of speed I preferred not to think about.

"What's this all about?" Tracy asked, bewildered.

"It's all about us getting a chance to talk, that's what, before the police get hold of us," Josh said grimly. "You don't think that bomb was any play toy, do you?"

Tracy gasped. "The Advocates for Children planted it. They must have!"

"Not necessarily." The words surprised me, emerging from my own lips, but I listened to them and agreed. "Tracy, that call you got said for you to be there at ten. We were there several minutes earlier. We weren't meant to be *in* the explosion, we were meant to *see* it! Or else we really *were* supposed to find the evidence, or whatever, that they promised. And the bomb was somebody else's dirty trick."

"What evidence?" Jeremy demanded.

Between us, Tracy and I recounted the

lead-up to our going to the plant. Jeremy's mouth tightened.

"You're right. We need to talk. Fast." He made an abrupt U-turn on the highway. "I'm taking you to my place, not the Kennedys'. The police have already questioned me, so they won't come there. They interviewed you two at the hospital, didn't they?" he asked Tracy, and she nodded. "Then our best chance for privacy is our house. See if you can locate Sam and Jen."

Tracy picked up the car phone and started trying numbers, while I huddled in Josh's arms and ignored the aching in my bones. At last she reached Jennifer, and, without giving her name, held the phone up to her brother.

Jeremy didn't identify himself either. "You know who's speaking? Just say yes or no." There was a brief pause while Jennifer was answering. "I have the kids. Yes, they're all right. I need you. Come to my place, both of you if possible, and don't wear a tail." He hung up.

"How did the ambulances know to come?" it finally occurred to me to ask. Jeremy, tight-lipped, told me that our anonymous tipster had struck again. A call had been received at the exhibition's sign-in desk, announcing that the evil Unicorn Unlimited plant had gone up in smoke.

"Only it didn't," Josh said. "Go up, I mean. Only the entryway was damaged."

"So far as we know," Jeremy said grimly. "The fire crew wouldn't let me go inside. I had to turn over my keys to them so they could inspect."

"We'll have to wait for another bulletin from our unknown correspondent," Tracy said in a high voice, and commenced to laugh and laugh. Josh and I looked at each other, and both of us were thinking the same thing. All these anonymous calls were a bit too much.

Come to think of it, the gambling raids that had precipitated Unicorn's troubles had also been triggered by an anonymous call.

A silence fell. The road was deserted, dark, and a gentle rain had begun to fall. At last a gatehouse loomed, and a man in a wet slicker shone a light at our faces and waved us through. We rolled past the gates along a curving drive and pulled into a garage beneath Jeremy Tyler's bachelor pad.

It was definitely a bachelor pad, even though he had a teenage sister living with him. The condo complex, all slate and weathered wood, sprawled over a hillside in such a way that the units seemed totally separate and secluded. Jeremy led us up cantilevered steps, and turned a key in the bronze Chinese lock on a dark carved door. We stepped inside, and I felt Josh's five senses coming to attention. I couldn't blame them.

There was a two-story-high living room, with a cathedral ceiling and sculptural chandelier. Underlit, cantilevered stair treads led to a balconied second floor. One wall of the living room was a fireplace, one was a media center; the sofa faced two directions to take in both of them, and was big enough for a sultan and his harem. A stand of bamboo, also lit from below, reached toward the ceiling, and ceiling-high windows, whole walls of them, looked out on the twinkling lights of the Santa Clara valley.

Jeremy pressed buttons on an elaborate alarm system built in by the door. Tracy looked at me wearily. "I don't know about you, but every inch of me aches. There's only one thing I want more than sleep, and that's the hot tub. I can loan you a bathing suit. We keep extras on hand for guests."

We both took showers first, for we were filthy from the explosion and the fire. Then, in a borrowed suit, I joined Josh and the Tylers and the Kennedys, who had come a little earlier, in the greenhouse hot tub. It was the first time I'd ever had a council of war in a hot tub. It was the first time I'd ever been *in* a hot tub, and I'd have either giggled or goggled if I hadn't been working so hard to stay awake. We each recounted the events of the evening as we recalled them, and a cassette recorder, placed prudently far from the water's edge, took them all in.

"Sidney's right. It could be the Advocates for Children's lunatic fringe, but not necessarily. The group is vehemently opposed to violence, after all," Jennifer said. She looked at Jeremy. "What did the police or fire crews tell you about the bomb?"

"They told me absolutely nothing," Jeremy

said flatly. "Maybe Hatch will find out more, but I doubt it. He's bound to be running around 'contacting his sources' by now. Or wheeling and dealing to shape the whole thing into a sob story that will win us public sympathy!" He sounded bitter.

I saw Josh's eyebrow go up.

"As your attorney, *I'll* contact the police the first thing in the morning," Jennifer said. "Not to mention putting a muzzle on Golden Boy. He should *not* be making statements to the press without benefit of counsel. We can probably count on Ellerbee to make him see reason in that respect." Her eyes narrowed. "Where is Ellerbee, anyway? He wasn't at the exhibition when we left. Did he go to the plant once the alarm went out?"

"Hatch did. Brian didn't. He probably got there after Josh and I left." Jeremy frowned. "Do we have to wait till morning to find out what the police have turned up so far?"

I remembered something I'd noticed earlier. "You have a CB radio, don't you? We could tune in the police frequency."

We picked up a dialogue between a patrol car and the police precinct house. The remnants of one bomb had been found just inside the main door to the plant. It had gone off at two minutes to ten, and the direct-line alarm system between the plant and the police station had reported it at once.

"So that's why the police and ambulance got there so fast," Josh said thoughtfully.

Jeremy gestured sharply for him to be quiet. The dialogue on the CB was crackling on. The search team had not yet turned up the timer and the detonating system used on the bomb. The lock on the main door, now in pieces, had not been tampered with, and the burglar alarm had not gone off. The team was now going to inspect the inside of the Unicorn plant. Over and out.

For a few minutes there was no sound except for the soft fizzing of the recirculating water in the hot tub. Then Jeremy turned to Josh and me with a drawn, set face. "I want you two to begin an investigation at once. For me, personally, not for Unicorn."

"Funny," Josh said deliberately. "We thought you didn't want us in on this."

"That was then. This is now. I should have listened to Sam and Jen in the first place, then maybe tonight could have been avoided. The full facilities of Unicorn will be at your disposal, but I don't want what you're doing to be known."

"We've already been offered a job," Josh said. Tracy's eyes flared in panic, but he went on smoothly. "Hatch and Ellerbee want to hire us to write a game for your Christmas line."

Jeremy nodded. "That will provide a good cover. I'll have an office set up for you at the plant — as soon as the plant's usable again, that is. We can make an announcement about your creating the game at the exhibition opening tomorrow."

I couldn't resist. "Positive publicity, as Mr. Hatch would say."

"And he'd be right." Jeremy looked from us to Jennifer. "Can we get a contract with these two negotiated and signed before the opening?"

"Let's get this very clear," Josh said carefully before Jennifer could speak. "You are engaging SSW Computer Enterprises to find out for you, personally, the following things: Who set that bomb off, and how, and why? Why Unicorn is being accused of marketing games for gambling and having a tie-in with organized crime, and who tipped off the police about that? And if there is any substance to the charges, who's responsible for getting Unicorn involved? In other words, who's been ripping you off, and how it was done. What effect is all this apt to have on your business? And what can you do right now to salvage the situation?"

"I couldn't have done a better summation for the jury myself," Jennifer murmured dryly. If Jeremy was amused by Josh's elaborate statement, he didn't show it. He simply said, "Yes."

"We're going to need —" I started to say. And stopped abruptly. Under the cover of the whirling foam, Josh had pinched me, hard.

"We can wait till morning to get into particulars," he said carelessly. "When we aren't all so tired. I don't think we'll have difficulty coming to terms for the contract, do you,

Webster? For the investigation, and the game."

I nodded. The hot water and dim lights were beginning to get to me, and I found myself starting to slide down beneath the foam. I was pulled out of my trance by two things. One was Josh's arms going around me to hold me tight. The other was an alarm that began a dull honking just before the doorbell began to ring imperiously.

Josh and I stared at each other, suddenly wide awake. Tracy started to pull herself from the tub, but Jeremy beat her to it. He was already tying a terry-cloth robe around him when a uniformed figure materialized against the glass door of the greenhouse room.

Jeremy unlocked the door and opened it, and the policeman stepped in, raindrops glistening on his coat.

"Jeremy Taylor? Lieutenant Carson would like to speak with you. The body of your partner, Brian Ellerbee, has just been recovered in the fire debris at the Unicorn plant."

Chapter 11

It was hours later before we got to sleep that night. The police talked to Jeremy, they talked to Josh, and to me. Each of us separately. When they were through with Jeremy, Jennifer started with him, briefly. Then she ordered Jeremy and Tracy to go to bed. To sleep, if possible — without worrying, also if possible. Then the Kennedys took Josh and me home, and Jennifer issued us the same orders. At which point Sam told her to follow her own prescription, and marched her off.

Josh looked at me. "I'm too beat to make sense now, anyway. First thing in the morning, okay?" He disappeared into his room, and I hit the sack.

I was awakened at five-thirty the next morning by Josh squeezing a wet washcloth directly on my face. Considering that I hadn't gone to sleep till after two, I was not thrilled.

"Too bad," Josh responded. His face looked serious. "We have to talk. Alone."

"Give me five minutes." I reached for my

robe, staggered into the bathroom, and took a very fast cold shower, which succeeded in making me wide awake though rather wobbly. When I went back to the bedroom, buttoning my robe, Josh was settled in the desk chair, fully dressed.

I pulled a chair up opposite him. "You want to start first, or shall I?"

"You."

"Why that long spiel to Jeremy Taylor, defining our job responsibilities? Or were you just showing off?"

"I wanted us to be covered, in case Tyler balks later," Josh replied. "Did you notice he very carefully avoided explaining why he hadn't wanted us to work for him before? Or why he wanted our working — for *him*, not the corporation — kept a secret?"

I frowned. "It sounds like he doesn't trust somebody in his company."

"Or he's afraid that he shouldn't trust somebody. He also," Josh added, "stayed way, way off the subject of that canceled game."

"Tracy didn't want us poking into that, either," I said slowly. "Interesting."

"Very. So interesting that maybe we'd better give that game some close attention. When we listen to that cassette," Josh said, "check out my wording of that 'show-off' speech. I was very careful with how I phrased it. We're covered if our digging around reveals a tie-in between that game rip-off and what's happening now."

"We'd better get a transcript of that

cassette, and fast. Not to mention working out terms for our contract. And figure out how we're going to get the answers to all those questions you dreamed up. And somewhere around the edges of all that, write a fantastic game." I started to giggle. "Do you realize we haven't even been here forty-eight hours, and we've already acquired two detective cases, been offered a job to write a computer game, gotten attention from the press, a grand total of eight hours sleep spread over two nights, initiation into hot-tub business conferences, and a bombing? We're going to need a vacation to get over our vacation!"

"It's not that funny," Josh said, and I replied, "I know," but I couldn't stop laughing. I also started to shake.

Josh regarded me with alarm. "Good lord, Webster. Hang on, I'll be right back." He vanished, and returned in a few minutes with coffee, orange juice, and a plate of bagels. "Eat," he ordered.

I took a long gulp of orange juice. "Like Dad said he learned in med school, 'Cut down on food or cut down on sleep, but not both at once.' What was on your list of things to settle?"

"Let's get back to the game question first." Josh heaped a bagel with cream cheese, and concentrated. "We'd better hold off any work on that till we get back home. Can you come up with some snappy idea that will satisfy Hatch, and keep Unicorn and the press off our backs till then? You should be able to come up with something before we meet with Jeremy this morning, can't you?"

I just looked at him. "Just spin them a million-dollar game concept off the top of my head? Out of thin air? Surely you jest. Or else you're out in orbit!"

Josh's eyebrows both rose. "Do my ears deceive me? Or is the great Sidney Webster actually admitting there's something her intuition cannot handle?"

"Leave my intuition out of this. You know as well as I do that if we're going to pull Unicorn out of the red and not fall on our faces, we have to come up with something that's more than good. That means research and hard work."

Josh ignored me. "Make it a text adventure game. Tyler likes them, and Unicorn doesn't have a good one yet. Text adventures sell like mad."

"You've discovered that, have you?"

Josh was off in the kind of game fog he'd so despised. "Something educational. Intellectual. But with lots of — What does Hatch keep calling it? Glitz." He sighed. "It really is too bad we can't really dazzle the press with something when the announcement's made. But of course, if you really can't come up with anything. . . ."

He left the sentence dangling tantalizingly.

The glint in his eyes was a challenge I could not resist. "King Arthur and the Round Table," I said sweetly. "That provides for castles and dragons and mythical adventures, which should make it not only popular, but practically a cult favorite with the college crowd. Plus plenty of blood and gore, and lust, and magic spells. Only King Arthur's knights were terribly high-minded, and it is a classic, so the Advocates for Children won't dare say a word. We'll call it *Excalibur*!"

"Fine," Josh said. "We've got a concept. Now you cook up the plot, I'll write the program, and we can knock the game off in a day or so."

"Not till we get back home," I said flatly. "We have enough troubles on our hands right now! I think we should bring in Cordelia and the hackers. We'll need all the information on Unicorn we can get."

Josh looked at me. "You know Tyler said we'd have full access, and his whole cooperation."

"A) He didn't say that where the pirated game's concerned. B) Do you honestly think the police are going to let *anybody* poke around Unicorn and its business records, let alone Ellerbee's? I'll bet they've already got everything sealed up tighter than a drum."

"We should worry," Josh said loftily. "We have a secret weapon. Speaking of which, we'd better reclaim Samantha as fast as we can without anybody asking questions. It'll take a while to crack into the Unicorn mainframe, and we'll have to work somewhere we can't be caught for hacking."

"You know the perfect place? The Tyler condo. Did you catch the way that warning alarm went off before the police approached? That place is even more of a fortress than this place is! And I can't believe Jeremy doesn't have his home computer wired into the Unicorn mainframe somehow."

Josh looked at me with respect. "You're right. See if you can maneuver work space there, while you're negotiating the contracts for the investigating and the game."

Brian Ellerbee had been so anxious to negotiate a contract for a game. A vision of the bombing rose vividly in my memory, with the image of Brian Ellerbee, dying, superimposed upon it. I flinched.

"*You* negotiate the contracts," I said brusquely. "You know what we need."

Josh shot me a worried look. "Do you feel okay? *You* always want to do the client deals. *You're* the one with the interpersonal relationship skills, remember?"

"Right now I've had enough of interpersonal relationships."

"Have another bagel," Josh said soothingly. "Okay, I'll tackle the contract and you can talk game concept with Mr. Public Relations Hatch."

"Don't do me any favors," I said bitterly.

It was now six o'clock, and we could hear the rest of the household stirring. I threw Josh out, and put on a good suit in preparation for the press announcement about our game. Anything to get good image back for Unicorn, I thought savagely, putting on eye shadow and pinning up my hair.

What was I being so resentful about, anyway? I wanted Unicorn to have its good image back. Not just for Josh's sake any longer, but for Jeremy's.

I took a long look at myself, let my hair down again, and wiped off half the blue eye shadow. They wanted innocent young girl, they'd get innocent young girl.

Maybe what I was so sore about was that I felt young and naive, and under the circumstances that was not only ego-deflating, it was scary.

I joined the others at the breakfast table, and a short while later went with Josh and Jennifer out to the Mercedes. Mike greeted me with a kind of wink, oddly intimate. I looked away quickly and got into the back seat, before anyone suggested I ride up front.

The hotel parking lot was jammed, and vans from two TV stations clogged the entrance. The Advocates for Children pickets were back in force, and uniformed policemen mingled discreetly with the crowds.

"Isn't there a back entrance? Get us around there," Jennifer said sharply. Mike swung out of the parking lot with a screech of brakes. He was some driver, I admitted grudgingly, and I was conscious of his shooting a macho look in my direction.

We tootled along and in the service road, Mike drew up beside trash bins in the rear.

"If you cut through those bushes you'll be on the jogging path that winds past the swimming pool. You can go in through the dressing rooms and take the elevator to the lobby."

So that was what we did. The pool, ringed with brown and white chaises and umbrella tables, would have looked inviting at any other time. Today, we just strode past. The elevator dumped us in the lobby and we went toward the rooms Sam's company had rented as an entertainment suite. Nobody pounced on us. The press apparently had not yet been allowed inside, and most people's attention was focused on a big-screen TV that was set up near the entrance to the exhibit hall.

Larger than life, a news program was displaying the footage taken last night of the Advocates for Children demonstration. There was Jennifer, looking assured, unworried, very much in command. There was Jeremy Tyler, looking desperately worried.

There was Josh, stooping swiftly toward the ground as the shoving match began. Looking for all the world as though he was ducking out, I thought, amused. Josh muttered something underneath his breath.

"What?" I hissed.

"Not now. Something I forgot to tell you. When we're alone."

The scene changed to that persistent reporter, trying to pin Jeremy down. Then to me, batting my eyes and putting on the Miss Innocence act, as Ellerbee tried to maneuver me about the game. I was profoundly grateful the camera did not reveal what I'd been really thinking.

All at once the bombing of the Unicorn plant flooded the screen.

"Sidney," Jennifer said, warningly. "Sidney, come. We'll be late for the contract talks."

"Josh is doing that," I said without moving. "Just bring me the papers when you have them ready, and I'll sign them."

I heard Jennifer and Josh move away.

It was weird, the explosion and the fire that followed had not hit me as hard last night as they did now, in big-screen living color. Maybe it was because I'd been in shock. Maybe it was because I knew now that Brian Ellerbee had been inside, dead.

Had been inside — ? What had made me think in just that way, as if I knew somehow that he'd died earlier, not in the bombing? I drew my breath in sharply.

The announcement of Ellerbee's "tragic death" under "unexplained circumstances" followed, and you could almost hear violins in the background. *Or was it the kind of screechy music-by-computer that suspense shows used to indicate skullduggery afoot?*

I was either getting spooked from lack of sleep, or my ESP was working. I didn't want brain waves right now, I wanted solid evidence of . . . what? I didn't know.

Conspiracy? Game piracy? Stock manipulation?

Murder?

Chapter 12

I jerked myself away from the TV, breathing hard, and streaked for the exhibition hall to see if there were any ground currents about Unicorn I could pick up in the crowd.

There were plenty of currents floating, and plenty of rumors. After an hour of furtive looks in my direction, conversations quickly hushed when I was recognized, and "absolute facts" about everything, I didn't know which to be more — furious or worried.

"Ah, Miss Webster, there you are!" Ivan Hatch bore down on me, flashing his toothpaste smile, with Josh behind him. "All ready for the big announcement? If you'll just put your John Hancock on the dotted line, we'll be ready for you two people to meet the press."

He hurried Josh and me to the meeting room that had been designated for the press. I barely had time to read the contracts through, and scribble my name as president of SSW Enterprises, before the TV lights impaled me.

It was a situation fraught with pitfalls, but Ivan Hatch kept a firm command. He refused to comment on the bombing or Ellerbee's death, and kept the interview firmly on the matter of the game SSW Enterprises had just signed to write for Unicorn.

"It will be on the market in time for Christmas giving. A text-adventure game — something quite different for Unicorn, and it will be specially designed to be appropriate and appealing for all ages! That's right — *Excalibur*!" He leaned heavily on the game's educational aspects and our wholesome ones. I smiled sweetly, and watched my words just as carefully, and gagged inside.

I got off the hook finally because one of the exhibit guides arrived to say there was a telephone call for me. "And they say it's urgent."

I took the call on the phone at the SMN booth. "Sidney! We just saw the newsreels of the bombing. Are you all right?" That was my father, and my mother was on the extension, saying anxiously, "I think you should come home."

"I'm fine. We're both fine." I kept my voice very neutral, because there were people around the booth. "Dad, Thor's friend and his wife are looking after us beautifully. Guess what? We just signed up to write a computer game."

"For Unicorn? Are you two investigating

that?" Dad could add two and two as well as anyone. "Sidney, do be careful. Maybe you should come home."

"*No!* I can't talk now. I'll call you. Call Josh's mom and tell her we're okay." I hung up before my parents could protest.

Whether Josh was still in being interviewed, I didn't know. He wasn't near me. I went wandering again, collecting two shopping bags full of giveaways. By two o'clock I realized I hadn't had lunch and my lack of sleep was catching up with me again.

I headed for the coffee shop off the lobby. The lunch crowd was starting to thin out. I started toward a booth in the back corner. I was halfway there when a voice stopped me. It belonged to Aldous P. Shuttleworth, and it was saying, "My dear Miss Webster, won't you join me?"

He was sitting at a table on the aisle, halfway through his meal. I did a double take, and then said distantly, "No, thank you." And started on. At least I thought that was what I was doing. Only instead I found myself being inserted in a chair by Mr. Shuttleworth, who had bounced to his feet with speed surprising for one his size and weight.

"Waitress! What will you have, my dear? It's my treat. I insist."

"I don't want anything," I said distinctly.

"But I do," Mr. Shuttleworth said, with his grandfatherly smile. He waved the waitress off with instructions to come back in five minutes.

"Mr. Shuttleworth," I said carefully, "what is this all about?"

"Just a little conversation, that's all. Your parents aren't here at the exhibit with you, are they? Don't you think it would be wise to consult them before getting yourself entangled with Tyler and his crowd?"

"Why?" I demanded baldly.

Shuttleworth looked, for once, at a loss for words. "Because that company isn't fit. My dear Miss Sidney — I may call you Sidney, mayn't I? I'm old enough to be your grandfather, and wiser than you in the jungle of the business world. You're a very young girl, my dear, and it's really not suitable that you should allow the . . . taint of that company's criminal connections a chance to soil you. I'm sure if your father were here —"

"My father," I interrupted, "has respect for my judgment. He also taught me not to make prejudicial judgments without having all the facts."

"What facts?" Something changed in Shuttleworth's eyes. "If you have any evidence concerning Unicorn Unlimited, young lady, you have a duty to turn it over to the authorities. In fact I strongly advise you to confide it to me right now, and *I* will take the proper steps on your behalf. You're getting yourself involved in something much more serious than you realize, and your youth and innocence are no protection from the dangers."

All at once I felt a shaking starting, deep within me. My voice didn't shake. I was very proud that I did not allow my voice to shake. "It certainly didn't protect me last night, did it?" I said icily. "And I can assure you, Mr. Shuttleworth, that *if and when* I come up with any evidence about the Unicorn bombing and Mr. Ellerbee's death, I'll go straight to the authorities with it myself."

His eyes changed again. Either he was the world's best actor, or he was genuinely shocked. "My dear, you don't think — Miss Webster, the Advocates for Children are fundamentally opposed to violence. Please tell Mr. Tyler that. He can check our record. We will use every peaceful means at our disposal, even civil disobedience if necessary, to rid the world of the filth he and his kind expose children to, but we do not and will not participate in or condone the kind of violence that took place at the Unicorn plant last night. You must tell him that!"

Out of the corner of my eye I saw the waitress coming nearer. "I'll tell him," I gabbled, and got out of there. Fast.

I plunged back into the crowds of the main exhibit hall, and when I spotted Josh, I couldn't help myself. I grabbed his arm.

"What's up?" Josh looked surprised and, when he saw my face, alarmed.

"Not now. Take me someplace where I can get something to eat, will you?"

Josh asked no questions, just took both my

bags in one hand and put the other arm protectively around me. "We can get lunch on the terrace out by the pool."

The sun had gone in, and the sky looked stormy. Because of that, and the late hour, the terrace was deserted. Josh parked me at an umbrella table that had no one near it, and went to find a waitress he could hassle.

He came back to announce that hamburgers were on the way. "In the meantime, tell me what happened," he demanded.

"Aldous P. Shuttleworth is what. He wanted to warn me against working for Unicorn. Something about how the evilness of the company would corrupt my purity. Josh, stop laughing. I know it sounds funny, but it didn't when he said it."

Josh's face tightened. "What else did he say?"

"He wanted to buy me lunch, if you'd believe it. And then he —" I frowned. "Josh, he asked me what *proof* I had about *Numero Uno* being written for the gambling syndicate." I related the rest of the conversation swiftly. "It was almost as if he were threatening me. And then suddenly turned sweet as pie and wanted me to take a message to Jeremy."

The waitress arrived with our orders. We shut up till she was gone.

"I think," Josh said carefully when we were again alone, "I know what Shuttleworth was getting at. I was wondering when he'd put two and two together."

"Put two and two together about what?"

"What became of that evidence he was waving around before the TV cameras yesterday." Josh looked complacent. "In all the excitement about the bombing, I forgot to tell you. Remember when I ducked down during the demonstration? I pinched the game disk he'd been being such a pompous fool about."

"You *what?*"

"Pinched it," Josh said complacently. "Don't you remember how Shuttleworth wanted the reporters to check that one particular disk for evidence of the gambling tie-in? He dropped it when all the pushing and shoving started, and I happened to pick it up."

I eyed him. "Happened to, my foot. Which did you do, pick his pocket or start the shoving?"

"You don't want to know. The way I see it," Josh said around bites of hamburger, "there must be something on that disk or Shuttleworth wouldn't have risked trying to demonstrate it on national TV. Once we see *what* it is, and *where* it is, we should be able to tell whether it's something the Advocates added to the disk themselves, or whether it's organic in the game itself."

"If somebody else didn't patch something into the program."

"In which case there ought to be evidence of the patch, and Samantha will find it." Josh frowned, looking at me with concern. "What's the matter with you, Webster? You aren't thinking this thing through."

"I'm tired, that's what. And this place is getting on my nerves." I took a gulp of coffee. It was bitter, but the warmth spread through my body. "I wish we could get away from here and log onto Samantha."

"We still have to collect her," Josh reminded.

"Maybe Sam would take us, if he's not too busy. Or Jennifer."

"Or Mike."

"Not Mike." I felt my face reddening, and went on quickly before Josh could ask questions. "That game disk you got off Shuttleworth — we don't *have* to wait till we have Samantha to check it out. We can ask the Tylers if we can take a cab to their place, and then check it on one of Jeremy's computers. Where's the game disk you lifted?"

"In my attache case," Josh said promptly. Then he froze, and his face went white.

"Josh, what is it?"

"Oh, lord, Webster," Josh whispered hoarsely, "I don't know. I had the attache case when Ross Taylor told me you'd left for Unicorn last night. After that it's a blank. I haven't a glimmer in hell of where either the attache case or the game disk is now!"

Chapter 13

For an instant we just stared at each other. I swallowed hard.

"Okay, let's retrace your steps. You were in the exhibit hall with your attache. Where were you?"

Josh thought hard. "At the IBM display, looking at their investment manager program. I had the attache case on the counter next to me."

"Then what?"

"Then Taylor came and told me about your taking off for Unicorn, and I did, too."

"Did you grab the attache case as you left?"

"I don't *know*! I never even thought of it again till now," Josh said starkly. "How could I have been such a fool!"

"Never mind that now. Maybe somebody turned it in to Lost and Found. Come on." Josh castigating himself for stupidity was so unnerving I was afraid to let him sink too far into it. I rushed for the hotel's front desk, forgetful of my own weariness, and Josh followed, carting my shopping bags of give-aways.

No one at the front desk knew anything about the attache. We were handed over from person to person, and finally to the manager himself. His word was final: The attache case had not been found by any employee, nor had it been turned in.

"Have you checked at the exhibition itself?" the manager asked. "It could have been turned in to your display booth, or at registration."

I shook my head. "We're not attached to a particular display. And there's no way anyone would know who the case belonged to."

"Yes, there is," Josh said bleakly. "Don't you remember the identification tags the airline handed out? I put one on the attache case, with my business card stuck in it. It seemed like a good idea at the time."

But not now. Those business cards, which we'd had printed up with a flush of self-satisfaction after our first case, did not just give our names. They said *SSW Enterprises, Computer Consultants.* Which could mean merely analysis of data and of business systems, but really meant much more — and an awful lot of people knew it. That attache case, identified with us, was also, thanks to Hatch & Ellerbee's little media blitz, identified with Unicorn Unlimited.

"We'd better check, anyway," Josh muttered. So we made the rounds of the exhibition: check-in desk, sponsors' reps, service areas, IBM and SMN and Unicorn, and everywhere else that we could think of. No one knew anything.

"Maybe we should call the police," I said thoughtfully. "If you did take it with you, you could have dropped it somewhere in the bomb debris." Then I stopped. "We're both being fools. *Ross.* If you had it when you left here, it's probably in his car."

Back to the lobby, both of us feeling sheepish but irrationally better. Digging out the phone numbers Ross had given us. Phoning from the lobby pay phones, on the theory that sometimes the greatest privacy was in a public place.

Ross wasn't at his hotel. He wasn't where he said he might be. I finally called my Aunt Jane's number in New York. She wasn't home.

"That's that," Josh said heavily. "The one blasted piece of evidence we've gotten in this whole lousy case, and it's gone."

"Don't. If there really is a gambling game in *Numero Uno*, it must be on more than one game disk."

"All we have to do is find which ones," Josh finished. "You are bearing in mind, aren't you, that the Unicorn crew has already gone over the master disks and all the merchandise waiting shipment in the warehouse?"

"They say they have."

"Meaning you think it could be an inside job? So do I," Josh said. "Come on."

We headed into the exhibition hall, which was now a madhouse. People kept stopping us to talk about our Unicorn game.

"Think good public image," I muttered to Josh, and turned on a plastic smile. Josh scowled, but kept his mouth shut. I made with the bright, noncommittal statements, and Josh with his arm around my waist kept easing me along.

"Here you are. I've been looking for you." It was that woman reporter from the network. "I'm interested in knowing more about this deal you've worked out with Unicorn Unlimited. Why should two smart kids like you sign with a company that's going down the drain?"

"We don't know it's going down the drain," Josh said, deceptively calm.

I could almost hear swords clashing.

The reporter switched subjects. "Did you come to California specifically to do work for Unicorn?"

I gave her a wide-eyed look. "We were only asked to write a game yesterday. While you were talking to me, wasn't it?"

"I wasn't referring to the game. Did you come out here to conduct an investigation into the Unicorn troubles for Jeremy Tyler, the way you were investigating The Joker's backstage sabotaging of *Lust for Life*, under the pretext of researching soap opera demographics for the producer?"

Josh's hand tightened, hard, at my waist.

I managed a girlish laugh.

"I'm a high school sophomore! Do you honestly think my parents would let me come cross-country on a — an undercover mission? This is our spring vacation, and we were offered a chance to come to this exhibition. On our own. That's all the excuse any high school couple needs!"

"You are a couple, then?" The reporter's tone was light, but not her eyes. I thought, *what do I do next?*

To my relief — and astonishment — Josh pulled me close. "What do *you* think?" he asked, with a convincing imitation of the tone Ross Taylor used when being macho in *Lust for Life*. Before I could expire from shock, he shepherded me back out to the terrace.

We found a deserted table and sat down. The sky by now was leaden. A muscle was working in Josh's left temple. He caught me looking, and we both turned scarlet and looked away.

"Thanks," I mumbled. "I'm sorry to put you through that."

"Think nothing of it," Josh said. There was a note in his voice that made my antennae go up in alarm.

"I'm sorry if I embarrassed you. I really appreciated you playing along."

"I usually do play along, don't I? Even though I don't like play-acting. But so long as you don't seem to mind it. . . . I figured," Josh said carefully, "that you would have no objections to my pawing you in public for a worthy cause, since you didn't seem to object to all-things-to-all-people Mike coming on to you."

All of a sudden the subject had shifted with a vengeance.

I stared at Josh, and all my pretenses fell away. "I hated it," I whispered. "When Mike came on to me, I was never so glad of anything as when you interfered. Only I couldn't say so, could I? For a lot of reasons."

Josh was standing very still, and breathing hard. "I'd never been so angry in my life," he said slowly. "Me. The nonemotional, as you would say. When I saw him — showing off for you like that, I saw red. I told myself I interfered because he could be dangerous, but that wasn't it. It was because I couldn't stand to see *him* touching *you*."

I wasn't breathing any too well myself. "I couldn't stand it either," I said. "I let him, because I thought maybe I could get some information out of him that way. I don't like pretending things any more than you do. I suppose we have to, sometimes, if we're going to be detectives. But I — I hated it just now, having to — you know, fake a love scene for the benefit of the press to keep them off the track."

"Who said I was faking?" Josh asked huskily. And leaned in.

The kiss he gave me was very satisfactorily not fake. Neither was the one I gave him back. We didn't have much chance to really get into things, though, because Jeremy Tyler interrupted us. His voice did, rather, for we were too preoccupied to notice his approach.

"I've been trying to locate you. That fellow Taylor called. He says he has something that belongs to you, and he has to talk to you when he returns it — somewhere private. I need to talk to you both in private, too. My car's out front. I told Taylor to meet us at my condo."

The attache case. Josh's eyes met mine and with one accord we broke out of our clinch and started after him.

Only we didn't get far. We were stopped, midway on the path to the hotel, by the detective who had talked to me last night. He was flanked by two uniformed policemen, and the dialogue was all too terribly out of TV detective series reruns.

"Mr. Tyler, I'm afraid we'll have to ask you to come with us. There are some questions we'd like to have you answer."

"I told you everything I knew last night," Jeremy said curtly.

"There are some further elements in the case that we didn't know of then. Now if you'll just come along. I'm sure you don't want to make this any more difficult than it has to be."

"You have no idea," Jeremy said deliberately, "how difficult I intend to make things unless I know exactly what is going on."

The detective shifted his attack, as I'd seen Ross Taylor do in a dramatic scene. "Did you know that your partner Brian Ellerbee had been manipulating sales of stock in Unicorn Unlimited in such a way that at the time of his death he owned more than twice as much as he had a year ago?"

Jeremy was jolted. We all saw it. "There surely is a logical explanation," he said at last.

"Sure. And the most logical I can think of is that he was pulling a fast one on you, and he may have been behind the other troubles Unicorn is in now. The gambling business. He could have rigged that to drive stock prices down, so he could buy a lot of stock up cheap. Maybe more shares than you own, yourself. And maybe you found out and decided to do something about it," the detective said.

"If you're suggesting I bombed my own plant," Jeremy said coolly, "that's ludicrous."

"We'd love to have you prove that to us, Mr. Tyler. At the station."

"Just a moment, Lieutenant. Are you placing me under arrest? Because if so, I have a right to know the charges and to have my lawyer present."

The lieutenant shrugged easily. "Who's talking about arrest? We're just taking you in for questioning."

"And I decline to oblige unless you have made a formal charge. For which I know perfectly well you have insufficient grounds."

A distant thunder rumbled. Everyone ignored it. Everyone was being terribly laid-back and calm, and my heart was thumping.

"I told you there were further developments," the lieutenant said pleasantly. "One is Ellerbee's stock manipulations. Two is the fact that Ellerbee didn't die in the bombing. He was already dead. Three, of all the people involved with Unicorn's problems, you're the only one who has no witness to your whereabouts at the times Ellerbee died and the bomb went off. You seem to have simply vanished for some considerable time yesterday. And four, Ellerbee left here after receiving a message from you to meet him at the Unicorn plant."

"*What?*"

"A message on the computer at the Unicorn desk. Two of your customers saw it on the monitor, and Ellerbee commented about it to them. He said it had to have actually come from you, because it was logged in with your private code number. So if you still insist we place you under arrest before you'll answer questions, Mr. Tyler, we'll be happy to oblige. We have more than enough to charge you with suspicion of murder."

Chapter 14

"Tell my sister!" Jeremy shouted back as they marched him off. "And send my lawyer!" So we did. Jennifer took off like a guided missile for the police station, and Tracy went stiff and cold.

She was in shock, I knew. I put my arms around her, and when she started shaking Josh said very calmly, "Tracy, do you have the keys to your brother's car? Give them to me."

Tracy seemed not to hear. I looked at Josh. "What do you think you're going to do?"

"Drive her home. She's in no shape to drive herself. Besides, are you forgetting Ross will be waiting for us?"

"You don't have a license!"

"Yes, I do." Josh was matter-of-fact. "I haven't used it since we moved to Lakeland, because New Jersey has a seventeen-year-old minimum age. But California doesn't. Now, will you find those keys so we can get out of here?"

When was I going to stop being surprised by Josh's hidden talents, I wondered bewilderedly, fishing through Tracy's bag. I found keys with a Jaguar tag, and Josh went to get the car while I told Sam what was up.

Sam's calm didn't crack. "You two had better stay with Tracy till Jennifer gets back with news. She may not be able to get Jeremy out on bail very quickly."

I stared at him. "You don't sound surprised by any of this!"

"I'm not. I think Jer's been set up." He gave me a penetrating look. "You two youngsters are in a position to make full use of your talents, and you'd better do so. All my resources are at your disposal. You don't have to ask." He strode away before I could ask any questions.

I went back to the chair where I'd parked Tracy very thoughtfully. It wasn't like Sam to refer to us by that patronizing "youngsters," and it could mean one thing only. Sam was telling us that being unofficial, being under age, Josh and I were in a position to ask and do things he, Jennifer, even the police, could not — at least not without a lot of red tape.

He meant hacking. He meant he'd better not know what we were up to. He meant not only Samantha, but all the rest of SMN's resources could be used without asking his permission.

Tracy was beginning to come back to life. I steered her out the back way through the bushes to where Josh and the Jag were waiting. We scooted out the service exit to avoid publicity.

Josh sent the black Jag purring along the freeway. It was late afternoon now, but it looked like dusk, and wind tossed the trees. The storm was drawing closer. The slate and wood of the condo complex glowed bleakly through the gloom. At the entrance gate the attendant (armed, I noticed) glanced into the car, recognized Tracy, and waved us through.

Tracy found her keys and unlocked the carved front door. "It's cold. Light a fire, will you, somebody?" She drifted off like a sleepwalker toward her bedroom. Josh and I exchanged glances, and I followed.

"Look, if you want to scream or cry, go ahead. We won't blame you."

"I can't," Tracy said tiredly. "Anyway, it wouldn't help my brother. Look, just give me an hour alone, will you? I feel as if I haven't slept for weeks. After that we'd better talk. . . . I wish you'd both stay here. The living room has every imaginable computer equipment you can use."

Josh had thrown logs into the open firepit. He struck a match, and flames flared up toward the copper hood. The glass doors to the deck were ajar, and cold air ran its fingers down my neck. I shivered and closed the doors, and lit a low lamp.

When the intercom bleeped I almost screamed.

It was the gate attendant, announcing Ross's arrival. I said he was expected.

A few minutes later the warning alarms on the deck railings sounded, and the doorbell rang. Josh opened the door, and Ross came in. Josh's attache case dangled from his hand.

"You left this behind, so I thought I'd better run it over." Ross set the attache case in the center of the coffee table. "This was *not* in my car when I left the Unicorn plant after the bombing. I know that for an absolute fact, because by the time I went back to the car after prowling around with the camera crew, my shoes were covered with mud. I have a rented car with pale beige carpet, and I didn't want to make a mess. I remembered having some newspapers in the back seat, so I put the light on and looked for them. They were there, and that was all. That's why I can be so certain the attache case wasn't there."

"But you have it now." It was Josh who said that.

"We've been shooting on location all day," Ross said. "When I left the shoot an hour ago, I opened the back car door to toss in the two-suiter I'd taken with me. I'd taken that because this morning I couldn't find the flight bag I generally cart personal items and scripts around in. I assumed I'd probably left it one of the places we'd been photographing. When I looked in the back seat, the flight bag was on the floor where I'd expected it to be. And that attache case was in the middle of the back seat."

It could have been a time bomb the way Josh and I stared at it, squatting enigmatically in the middle of the driftwood table.

"Let me get this straight," Josh said slowly. "Your flight bag was taken from your rental car while it was parked at Unicorn when you drove me there. And my attache case must have been taken from there, too." He spun the combination locks rapidly, his eyes intent.

The case flew open. Josh's notebooks and papers lay in their usual orderly piles. He manipulated the inner lid and it, too, sprung open. "Thank goodness for secret compartments," Josh breathed fervently.

He took out a plain, unlabeled six-inch square white envelope, open at one end. Inside was an innocuous looking computer disk bearing the label, *Numero Uno.*

Josh and I looked at each other. "This has to be the one I put in here. And not tampered with," Josh told me. "Nobody's been in the secret compartment since I closed it last. I have ways of knowing."

"What *I* want to know," I said slowly, "is how somebody knew to swipe the attache case in the first place. How did they know you had that thing?"

"Obviously, I wasn't as smart as I thought I was," Josh answered tautly. "Somebody must have seen me lift it."

"And known to look for it in your attache case in Ross's car? Somebody must have followed you to the Unicorn plant that night."

"Or been there already, waiting for the bomb to go off," Josh said deliberately.

The air was electric, and not just from the approaching storm. Ross, diplomatically, moved toward the door.

"I have to be going. I have an early call, and I'll be taking the afternoon flight back to New York. If there's anything I can do for you in the meantime, call me."

I saw him to the door. When I came back Josh had lit more lamps and was exploring the room for its electronic gadgets. At last he found a button concealed in the driftwood table, and the burled wood paneling on the opposite wall slid open.

Inside was an entire electronics center: big-screen TV, two smaller sets, floor-to-ceiling components of radio, tape decks, laser disk player, and VCR. And three computers.

"Tracy wasn't kidding. This place is fully equipped. I wonder which computer this game's programmed for? Too bad we don't have Samantha handy," Josh muttered. Samantha was compatible with *everything*. He tried the IBM first. Incompatible. Then he tried the newest Apple. *Numero Uno* flashed up on the screen.

At first it looked completely innocent.

"The best way to check a game is to play it," I pointed out. I started to pull a chair up to the keyboard, but Josh beat me to it, keyboarding like an addict. I blinked. Josh obviously *had* been boning up on game playing. I magnanimously refrained from comment.

After several minutes Josh said tightly, "Webster. Take a look at this."

I stared over his shoulder and frowned. "Something's weird. It's almost like the *Numero Uno* game I've played, but I've never seen those particular symbols or terms before."

"Know what they mean?"

"No."

"Let's look at them blown up. Tyler must have a set-up to rig his computers to that big TV screen." Josh fiddled around, and a short while later *Numero Uno* loomed four feet high.

I heard a gasp behind us. Tracy stood there in a green velour robe, staring. "I know what those terms mean," she said, her voice carefully even. "I went with Jer to a computer show in Las Vegas last year. What you're looking at is an illegal gambling game, exactly the way Aldous P. Shuttleworth said."

Chapter 15

Tracy came toward us slowly, drawn by the screen. "I don't understand. That's certainly not the way Jeremy programmed *Numero Uno*."

"But is it the way the *Numero Uno* games have been being manufactured? That's the main point," Josh said dryly. Tracy shook her head.

"As soon as the gambling charges came up, Jeremy checked the master disks himself. Nothing's been altered on them."

"Then somebody's been altering game disks after they've been manufactured." Josh frowned. "But how?"

"Maybe Samantha can find out. We have to get her back, and fast." I picked up the phone, but Josh stopped me.

"Wait a minute." He hauled out of his attache case's secret compartment a gadget I knew well. It was for detecting taps on telephones, and Josh checked all the phones before he let me use one. Then I telephoned the police station, and by luck Jennifer was still there.

"Jen, it's me. We're at Tracy's, and we need Samantha badly. Can you get her, yourself, without *anybody* knowing?" I hoped I wouldn't have to explain what I meant by that. As it turned out, I didn't.

"Yes. It's better if no one's in a position of being asked to give evidence. *I* won't have to, because of a lawyer's rule of confidentiality. I'll bring Samantha myself, within an hour," Jennifer promised, and hung up.

While we were waiting Tracy took a casserole from the freezer and heated it in the microwave. We ate around the fire while we watched the evening news. It was not, to say the least, encouraging to the digestion.

First we saw the full spectacle of Jeremy's arrest, from his departure from the hotel to his arrival at the police station. Then the lieutenant bragged a little about it, looking full of secrets but actually telling nothing. Then we were treated to Aldous P. Shuttleworth, looking solemn, resolute, and profoundly shocked. To juice up the rest of the broadcast, the network brought in financial news reporters to discuss the imminent demise of Unicorn Unlimited.

Josh flicked the set off abruptly.

The fire died down, and the sky darkened, and a car drove into the driveway beneath the balcony. The doorbell rang, and it was Jennifer, lugging the boxes that contained Samantha. "I have a key card, you know, to where this was. Sam had her already packed up for you, as it turned out. He won't mind my making the delivery. I'll tell him I did so, later."

"Were you followed?" Josh demanded. Jennifer shook her head.

"I'd take my oath on it. I came in my car, not the Mercedes, and I watched through the rearview mirror constantly. I thought something like that might be going on."

She could tell us very little more than we knew already, and she soon left. Josh assembled Samantha and booted her up. Tracy looked startled.

"You didn't have to send for your own computer. You could have used ours."

"This one's faster," Josh muttered and added, with his usual tact, "Why don't you go to bed?"

"I'm staying. I hired you first, and I own a large chunk of Unicorn, remember?" Tracy retorted firmly.

I told Samantha to make several printouts of the entire doctored *Numero Uno* game disk, and while she was at it to see if she could spot the changes. Samantha did her version of a falsetto purr and blinked her lights, and Jeremy's printer started rattling.

We all scanned the printouts somberly. There was no doubt about it. Now that we had Tracy to translate gambling lingo, we could see clearly how a gambling syndicate could find these game disks very profitable. The question was how they'd gotten the disks, and whether anyone from Unicorn was involved.

Josh turned to Tracy. "I know your brother checked the game masters. I want to, too. Maybe our computer can find something that he missed. Can you get them, or do the police have them impounded?"

In answer, Tracy went to a concealed wall safe. "Jeremy brought them home as soon as he had checked them. He thought they were safer here." She held them out to Josh.

Samantha checked them. They were clean.

"At least they weren't destroyed in the bombing. I wonder if the police know that," Josh said thoughtfully.

"If you're going to start hacking, I *had* better go to bed. If I'm called as a witness, it will be better if I don't know anything." Tracy left.

Thunder crackled distantly.

"We may have to call in the hackers if we run short on time. But at least we're right here on location. Let's get started." Josh hauled out his little black book, and as fast as he came up with anything he dumped it into memory and I printed it out.

He cracked the local police records first. There were several pieces of information they had not shared with Jennifer.

They knew how the bomb had gone off. It was a sophisticated device that could have been planted any time in advance and had been activated by computer.

It had been planted directly in the front

entrance, where the least damage could take place, and had been scheduled for a time when no one should be around, so quite probably no one had been meant to be hurt. That meant the Advocates for Children might be involved, but the police thought otherwise.

The room where the master game disks were stored had not been affected by the blast. The police had been inside. They knew the *Numero Uno* disks were missing.

They knew Brian Ellerbee had died of a blow on the head, about five minutes before the bomb went off. There was no evidence of the body having been moved, and he had been found just inside the lobby, only ten feet removed from the bomb's effects.

I looked at this data on the big screen, and started to shake. "He must have been killed just before Tracy and I arrived. The murderer must have still been there!"

"That," Josh said, "explains how my attache case disappeared. The guy must have mingled with the crowd, once the emergency trucks arrived, and just slipped away."

"What was Ellerbee doing there?"

"Maybe trying to catch him?"

Our eyes locked.

"We have to get into Unicorn's records," Josh said abruptly. "Fast. Without anybody knowing. Before the police get into them, or let anyone else do so. Tyler accesses the Unicorn mainframe from here, so Samantha should be able to do it, too." He started poking around behind the Tyler hardware, and soon had Samantha wired in. "If we only didn't have to waste time trying to crack his code."

"If I needed a secret code number, I know what I'd use. The date I set up SSW Enterprises." I went into Tracy's darkened bedroom and shook her shoulders.

"Wake up. It's important. Do you know your brother's code for accessing the Unicorn mainframe? Then what's the date of Unicorn's incorporation, do you know? The exact day and month. I know the year."

Tracy rubbed her eyes. "August eighteenth."

"Are you sure?"

"Positive. It's my birthday. Jeremy gave me a block of Unicorn stock as a birthday present."

I took Jeremy's birth date, too, just in case, and rushed back inside.

My first guess had been right. As soon as I keyboarded the incorporation date, the Unicorn mainframe opened to us on the giant screen.

"Now if we just had that detecting program you wrote," Josh muttered, "it would save some time."

"In a cardboard slipcase in my shoulder bag. Get it, will you?"

"You did come to California prepared, didn't you?" Josh asked dryly, rummaging.

"Just like you did with the wiretap detector. We were hoping we'd wind up here in the condo, so I brought it with me today, just in case." I booted the program into Samantha and told her to produce all Unicorn employee records dating back to the company founding, also a list of all past and present stockholders, and make it snappy.

HASTE MAKES WASTE, Samantha informed me, flouncing.

"Save the sarcasm, this is a matter of life and death."

YOU CATCH MORE FLIES WITH HONEY THAN WITH VINEGAR, Samantha answered sweetly. Josh hooted.

"I don't want to catch flies, I want to catch a murderer. Samantha, please!"

Samantha, mollified, purred away and presently began to spit out printouts.

"I didn't know they'd had this many employees, let alone stockholders! We're going to suffocate in paper!" Josh groaned.

"Samantha! Pull employment records and stock transaction records for the following people: Tyler, Jeremy; Tyler, Tracy; Ellerbee, Brian; Hatch, Ivan."

"And any common link between employees and stockholders of Unicorn and employees and stockholders of SMN," Josh chimed in. "*You* ought to know how to access SMN," he reminded Samantha pointedly. "It's your home nursery!"

Samantha chattered at him, and the big screen blacked out, then sprang to life.

Josh whistled. I felt queasy.

"So Ellerbee *has* been buying and selling Unicorn stock like mad," Josh said thoughtfully. "No wonder the police think Tyler had a motive! And Hatch doesn't own nearly as much of Unicorn as he's supposed to. He was selling like mad up till six months ago."

"He's been selling some of it to Ellerbee," I said slowly. "The stock certificate numbers match up, see? If Ellerbee had gotten his hands on the rest of Hatch's stock — he wouldn't even have had to buy it, just have a way to force Hatch to vote the way *he* wanted. He'd have had more voting shares than Jeremy. He could have forced Jeremy out if he'd wanted to."

"Don't forget Tracy's stock. She'd have sided with her brother."

"I wonder if there's any other stockholder Ellerbee might have hoped to put a squeeze on. Samantha, what about those correlations? What did you find?"

Samantha's lights rippled, and so did the image on the screen. More names and numbers emerged. I peered, and stiffened.

"Well, well," Josh said inscrutably. "So our laid-back Lothario owns Unicorn stock. I wonder how he could afford it on a go-fer's salary. And nobody bothered to tell us Mike Kubiczek used to work for Unicorn before he attached himself to Sam!"

Chapter 16

Josh and I hacked all night, or near enough. We hacked into records on Aldous P. Shuttleworth and the Advocates, but didn't turn up anything suspicious. Then we hacked the backgrounds of Ivan Hatch and Brian Ellerbee, and things got interesting.

Both of them, Samantha told us, had sold Unicorn stock more than once just before bad news about Unicorn hit the fan. Ellerbee usually bought a lot of stock afterwards, while the price was low. Even more fascinating was that Ellerbee's telephone bills showed that he'd made calls to Aldous P. *and* the Dade County, Florida sheriff's office.

"So he's the rat," Josh said slowly. "Trying to drive Unicorn's value down so he could buy Tyler out — that's what he was up to!"

"That's not going to help Jeremy," I said gloomily. "It just gives him a motive."

At some point during the night I wandered into Tracy's room and fell asleep on the other twin bed. At some later point I woke up, wandered out, and found Josh still on the computer. "Find anything?" I asked drowsily, and Josh, without looking up, answered, "Not the links we need. There's got to be a key piece missing somewhere."

"I think I'll phone Ceegee in the morning and have him hack around on this whole crowd. He has sources *nobody* knows about."

Josh looked at his watch. "It's four-thirty A.M., which means seven-thirty back home. Why don't you call him now?"

Fortunately Ceegee himself answered. "Sure. Glad for the job," he answered promptly "Is this confidential, or do you want Steve and Cordelia in on it, too?"

"It's confidential, and I want them in. Tell Cordelia to find out everything she can about these people." I gave him a list of names. "Rumors, too. She can start by checking old computing magazines and newsletters. Josh's mother will help her round them up. Now rig up a modem, and I'll transmit a list of Unicorn employees for you to check. Use every computer number you've ever stolen, and *don't* leave evidence of a crack-in! I'll get back to you tonight to see what you've found."

"I hope you guys have a checkbook handy," Ceegee said happily. "And a lawyer. Have Samantha call my Apple in ten minutes and zap your lists." Being authorized to go hacking made him feel like Christmas.

It was now five A.M. Josh stifled a yawn. "I'm for the Jacuzzi. How about you?"

So pretty soon there we were, soaking in clouds of steam, sipping coffee Josh made, and watching a misty dawn. Business conferences at home were never like this. After a while Josh's voice got faraway, and I was sliding down beneath foam and steam.

The next thing I knew Josh had hauled me out and wrapped me in a towel and was shaking me with alarm. "Webster! Come back! Did you pass out or did you fall asleep?"

"Neither. I was concentrating," I said with dignity. Only my voice sounded kind of funny. By then Josh was hugging me, and I just let him. And that's how Tracy found us some time later, looking anything but businesslike.

"Breakfast is ready," Tracy said, tactfully ignoring the love scene she'd interrupted. "Are you two going to stay here and work, or are you coming to the computer exhibit with me?"

Josh and I looked at her with alarm. "You're not going there today!"

"I have to. Ellerbee's dead, Jeremy's in jail, and I'm not going to let people think the Tylers are ashamed. Or that Unicorn's going down the drain. And I'm certainly not going to let Ivan Hatch try to capitalize on everything without being there to put a muzzle on him!" So that was that.

Josh stayed at the condo to compute. I went with Tracy, and it was truly awful. It started with the TV crews lying in wait for Tracy

135

with baited traps, and went downhill from there.

Tracy took her place at the Unicorn booth, and kept the Tyler banners flying. We met, briefly, in the coffee shop for lunch. Other than that, I circulated until, by mid-afternoon, I was wiped out. I found a chair in an out-of-the-way corner and eased my feet out of my shoes. I rubbed one shoulder absently, and all of a sudden someone else's hand had come down over mine.

Mike Kubiczek had come up behind me and, without asking, began to give my shoulders a massage. I tried to move away, and my shoulders were gripped and held.

"Just relax. I'm good at this. I'm good at a lot of things, and it might be worth your while to find them out."

"I'm not particularly interested," I said frigidly.

"You should be. What *are* you interested in?" His voice had that uncomfortable intimate tone, with an added twist. His hands started rubbing again, then stopped, with his thumbs hard between my shoulder blades. "You're poking into the Unicorn case, aren't you? I thought you and the boyfriend were here for the 'rest and recreation.'" I writhed inwardly at the implication in his tone. "If you aren't working for Tyler as a private eye, why are you poking into his affairs? Or is it Tyler and affairs that interest you, not work?"

All at once I wasn't frozen anymore. I was

thrusting my feet, fast, inside my shoes and striding off. It was not a graceful exit, but I could not afford to worry about what Mike would make of it.

I made for the one place he couldn't follow me — the ladies' room. Fortunately, it was empty. I gripped the edges of the marble dressing table counter, and leaned forward, breathing hard. After a few minutes I heard the door behind me open.

"Are you all right?" It was Tracy.

"I'm fine. Just tired."

"I saw you with Mike Kubiczek. Has he been coming on to you?" I didn't answer, and Tracy came over, took hold of me, and turned me around to face her.

"Sidney, don't listen to him. About anything! He can take anything good, and twist it round and make it dirty. Just stay away from him! He thinks he's God's gift to women, and lots of them fall for him before they learn better. And once they do, he gets nasty."

"I have no intention of falling for him," I said vehemently. "And I'd be delighted to stay away from him if he'd just let me!"

"Now you're angry. I didn't mean to insult you." Tracy's arms fell. "I know *you'd* never fall for him; you've got something too good already. If I'd ever —" She stopped abruptly.

I stared at her, illuminated. "Did you —? Tracy, were *you* one of the women you were talking about? *Tell* me. It could be important!"

At last, haltingly, I got it out of her. "I was still only a kid. Oh, I should have known better, I suppose, but I'd never dated. Jeremy practically raised me, you know, since our parents died while he was in college. He was all wrapped up in Unicorn, and I was, too. I tagged along. . . . You know computer nerds," Tracy said tightly. "They never see girls as *girls*, especially somebody's kid sister. Mike treated me as . . . special. . . . I finally wised up and dumped him, and that's that. End of story." She wiped her eyes, and took a swift look in the mirror. "Are you ready to leave? We ought to go home and see how Josh is doing."

That obnoxious TV woman caught us in the hotel lobby. "Miss Tyler, your brother has been charged with first degree murder, and there are rumors that Unicorn will either have to be bought out or go out of business. Will you comment?"

"No comment," I snapped, and tried to maneuver Tracy away. Ears were flapping everywhere, and suddenly Tracy swung squarely toward the cameras, her color high.

"Yes, I do have a comment! Unicorn Unlimited is not up for grabs! The Tylers made it, and the Tylers will bring it back! If my brother's in jail, or —" She swallowed, and her eyes flashed green fire. "If my brother can't keep spearheading the company, *I'll* take over. I own a share of the company, and I've created games with Jeremy. And for your information, my brother has been framed. I know it, and I'm about to prove it!"

"You mean you have evidence of someone else's guilt?" the reporter demanded.

"Oh, I know who has a guilty conscience, and pretty soon the police will know, too," Tracy said enigmatically, and swept off, her head high.

We fell into the Jaguar amid astounded stares, including Mike's. Tracy gunned the engine, and we took off.

"That wasn't smart," I said at last.

"I don't care! Maybe I can't prove anything yet, but we will soon. I'm tired of everyone taking potshots at the Tylers!" She swung out on the highway along the cliffs at an alarming rate of speed.

I was going to be very glad to be back at the condo. *Maybe Ceegee's come up with something*, I thought hopefully. Maybe Josh has.

I wasn't thinking about much of anything, probably because of lack of sleep. So I really didn't notice much until it happened.

Just as we were going around a curve, a big red car zoomed out of nowhere, passing us, and knocking us toward the edge of the cliff. I heard the screech of metal against metal. Felt the sickening jolt. Smelled the burning rubber as Tracy, with a skill and swiftness I could scarcely appreciate till later, jerked the Jaguar back from the edge at the last split second and spun it around across the miraculously empty road, to come to a shuddering stop on the other side.

Chapter 17

"It was probably one of those crazy California drivers," Josh said casually, but his eyes were sober. This was when we were back at the condominium at last, Tracy still in shock, me making a fool of myself by falling into Josh's arms. "Let's not talk about it now. Dinner's ready. I made *cioppino*."

Josh was a cooking maven like my mother, and being turned loose on California seafood had inspired him. We ate, and talked about nothing much, and all the time I was conscious of putting off something I had to do. At last, when we were sitting somberly around the fire, I turned to Tracy.

"I'm sorry, but I have to know. You did let Mike in on that game you wrote with Jeremy, didn't you? That's why you didn't want us prying into it!"

Tracy's face flamed. She shot a frightened look in Josh's direction, then away. "I'm sorry," Josh said gruffly. "I can leave, but Sidney will tell me later anyway."

"No. Stay. I'd rather get it over .with,"

Tracy said in a low voice. "I never *gave* him the game. It was the first one I'd written, and I wanted to test it out, you know?" We nodded. "So one night I — I took the proto-type with me, and Mike and I played the game together in the car. That's all. He didn't make a copy. He didn't have the equipment to make a copy."

"And not long after that, you and Mike broke up."

"That's a kind way of putting it," Tracy whispered harshly. "He told me I was too much of a kid, that he needed a real woman. I guess he figured that would shut me up, and he was right. When the competing game showed up on the market, Jer fired Mike because one afternoon months before, he'd caught Mike sneaking out of a room where he'd had no right to be. Jer thought Mike had been in there stealing the prototype." She swallowed. "I finally told Jer Mike hadn't had a chance to steal the prototype because what he'd been doing in there was making out with me. Jeremy thought he'd been unfair to Mike, and got him the job with Sam. I never told him I'd played the game with Mike a few days after that. I was too ashamed."

That was that. I persuaded Tracy to go to bed. When I came back Josh was leaning against the fireplace's copper hood, staring at the flames as rain began falling beyond the blackened windows. I rubbed the back of my neck, and Josh came over and began to mas-sage my shoulders.

"How bad was it?" he asked.

"Bad enough. I was scared. Tracy's a fantastic driver, otherwise we'd be dead. I couldn't tell what kind of car sideswiped us, and I was too stunned to get the license number."

"We can go back in the morning and look at tire tracks."

"After this rain? And how can tire tracks tell us which car did it?" Then I did a double take. "So you *don't* believe that 'California hot-rodder' bit."

"What do you think?" Josh asked disgustedly. "Look, let's go out and check the Jag. Maybe there are paint marks."

The parking area of the condo complex was well lit. We picked our way cautiously down the rain-slick steps, and Josh carefully inspected the door on the passenger side.

"There's red paint in the scratches. A police analyst could identify the make of car. If we could only count on tire tracks!"

I stood motionless, staring at the Jaguar, and then I started to laugh. "You're the logician. What would you say were the odds on our having left tracks that will not wash out?"

"Webster, what is it?"

I pointed. "That's tar on the fenders. Inside and out." I felt, then held up sticky fingers. "It's still tacky. I remember, vaguely, hearing gravel fly up against the car just before the red car hit us. Maybe, just maybe, we both went through an area that had just been resurfaced! Wouldn't we both have left tar tracks on the highway?"

Josh hugged me. "We'll check it out, as soon as it's light!"

We went back inside, and celebrated with hot chocolate, and then Josh suggested it was long past time we got on the phone to Ceegee.

"Man, have we been busy!" Ceegee exulted. "I'll zap you everything by modem, and Cordelia's sent some photos and clippings by Express mail, but here're the high points. Something fishy's been going on at Unicorn for at least a year. The late Mr. Ellerbee was buying and selling stock like mad. And his buddy Hatch? Cordelia dug up some photographs of him. Hatch is quite a playboy. He likes to do his swinging in Las Vegas, and there are photos of him being very chummy with some well-known people."

"You mean like gamblers?"

"That's what I mean."

I almost dropped the telephone.

"Hang in there, Webster." Ceegee laughed. "I've saved the best for last. You know that character Kubiczek? Like, he's an employee of SMN and gets a salary that would keep me in hamburgers and milkshakes very nicely, but wouldn't allow for Hatch's kind of swinging."

"So?"

"So how come the guy has something like half a million dollars in the bank?"

"Find out!" Josh and I both yelled.

"Got it. Now rig your modem," Ceegee said patiently.

We rigged the modem, and Samantha had a lengthy chat with Ceegee's home computer.

"It will take too long to read printouts," Josh said. "Let's just add Ceegee's stuff to what Samantha's already been chewing over, and see what she makes of it. No, wait a minute!" He fished for his little black book of supposedly secret computer codes, and started hammering away at Samantha's keys.

"What are you doing?"

"Getting Kubiczek's income sources and bank and credit records. You don't want to know from where." He dumped the data into memory as fast as he retrieved it, then turned Samantha loose on it all.

Samantha chirped and purred; she growled a few times, and commenced flirting her red and green lights like mad.

"She likes it. She likes it." Josh was being supercool, but his hand gripped mine.

All of a sudden Samantha's deductions began showing up on the TV screen.

KUBICZEK, MICHAEL

He had two addresses, one an apartment in what we recognized was a rundown strip of Palo Alto, the other a Malibu beach house bought in the past year. He had been fired from Unicorn, from an unmagnificent salary, a few weeks after the date on which the look-alike of Unicorn's game had hit the stores. He'd started working for Sam, also for unmagnificent money, two months later. But four months before Jeremy had fired him, Mike had started receiving very magnificent money indeed. First in royalties from the competing game company. And during the past year in *very* large hunks of cash.

"Could be from the gambling syndicate," Josh commented. "They don't like to leave a paper trail for the police."

"Samantha! Where has he been spending money?" I blurted, and Samantha flashed an answer smugly.

IN MALIBU. IN MEXICO. IN LAS VEGAS. (!!!) ON THE BEACH HOUSE. ON CLOTHES AND COMPUTERS. ON WOMEN AND LIQUOR. ON THE RACE TRACK.

ON A TWO-DOOR CONVERTIBLE BRIGHT RED FERRARI.

"One thing's loud and clear," Josh said finally. "Something rotten's going on, even if murder wasn't part of it. . . . I don't much like the idea of having to tell Sam. Or Tracy."

"You don't have to tell me. I just read the screen." Tracy came in, her face set. "I can tell *you* something. That was a Ferrari that sideswiped us. I'd stake my life on it. Jer used to drag me to car shows when I was a kid and he was still indulging in wishful thinking."

I cleared my throat. "The sideswipe could have been an accident. It didn't *have* to have been Mike."

Tracy ignored that. She turned to Josh. "If

we can prove that the tire tracks you found matched Mike's car, and the paint on the Jag's scratches matches, too, that will be the hard evidence you were talking about, won't it?"

"That he sideswiped us, yes. Not that it was on purpose, nor that he's guilty of the other things your brother's being held for." Josh looked at me. "Isn't your ESP coming up with anything?"

"Something's nagging at me, but I don't know what."

Samantha groaned at me, and I touched her STORE button, then set the printer to spitting out the latest data. Outside the tall windows a breeze had sprung up, setting the trees shivering against the panes.

"I want to see the Ferrari," Tracy said stubbornly. "And that beach house!" Josh raised an eyebrow.

"They're in Malibu."

"I know that. I want to go. *Now*."

Josh and I exchanged glances. "Tracy," I said gently, "it's practically the middle of the night."

"If you won't come with me," Tracy said doggedly, "I'll go alone."

"Your car might not make it," Josh pointed out practically. "And the Jag's too noticeable."

Tracy ignored him and reached for the phone.

"Jen? I need a big favor. Can I borrow the Mercedes without anyone but you and Sam knowing about it? Not even Mike. We need to get something fast and have a computer with us, and we don't dare use the Jag." She told Jennifer briefly what had happened to us on the road. We heard Tracy draw her breath in sharply. "*No!* You *can't* come with us! You have to stay here because if we find something you'll have to act for Jeremy right away."

At last Tracy overrode Jennifer's alarmed objections. She hung up, and turned back to us grimly. "Jen's going to pick up the Mercedes from the hotel parking lot. She'll leave her own car there. We'll drive to her office in the Jag and swap cars with her. Mike won't think twice about Jeremy's lawyer having his car while he's in jail!"

"Just so he doesn't get a sudden impulse to drive down to Malibu himself!" Josh snorted, and refrained from pointing out to Tracy that the Mercedes would be as recognizable to Mike as the Jag would be. *But he wouldn't have any reason — that he knew of — to try to make Sam or Jennifer have an accident,* I thought, and felt a small bit safer.

"Sam and Mike are both spending the night at the hotel. Some old hacking buddies are in town from out of state, and they're all going to hang out together. Mike," Tracy said viciously, "will probably get plastered. Or for once I hope so!"

The parking lot was practically deserted, but it was well lit, and there was nobody in sight. Jennifer was waiting in the Mercedes. We changed cars, and Jennifer said anxiously, "Do get a good night's sleep before starting out!" We made ambiguous noises. We weren't telling her we planned to drive two hundred miles, and were starting now.

Tracy drove. Josh and I sat in back so we could operate the computer if we needed to. The car, a sleek, self-enclosed world, slid out onto the freeway. It seemed impossible we'd only been in California seventy-two hours. *We're really surpassing ourselves on this case,* I thought, and started to giggle helplessly.

An hour out on the road we stopped to eat. It wasn't elegant, but hamburgers and French fries had never tasted so good. Then we were on the road again. At some point I asked, "How long will it take to get there?" and Tracy answered, "Hours." And Josh said, practically, "We can't find out anything till daylight, anyway."

"Just pray the Ferrari's garaged there."

"It has to be," Tracy said. "He hasn't risked it up around Silicon Valley, or word would have gotten around that he'd acquired big money. It's a small world."

"I wish it was small enough for us to get more proof," I grumbled. Suspicions, not to mention not-quite-legally hacked evidence, were all well and good, but Jennifer couldn't get Jeremy released and Mike jailed on the strength of them.

We didn't just need proof Mike was throwing money around. We needed to prove how he'd gotten it, and to prove that was tied in with little things like a bombing, doctoring *Numero Uno*, selling same to the gambling syndicate, and murder.

It would all be easy for somebody who had Samantha, I thought idly. And that's when it hit me. Whole, and complete. It seemed both so unbelievable and so plausible that I didn't dare blurt it out aloud. Not yet.

With shaky fingers I got onto the computer and told it to locate Sam Kennedy.

The computer summoned him to the telephone in the hotel lounge; I could hear music playing in the background. "It's me. Don't mention my name," I said. "Just answer yes or no. Have you been or are you now, working on an invention that could be used to correct errors in software, or allow new material to be inserted, *after* the original manufacturing's finished? In a way that would leave the software still apparently new, untouched disks?"

I felt Josh snap to attention next to me. He reached over and punched on the phone's amplifier, so we all could hear Sam's answer.

"Yes."

"Does anyone know about it?"

"No."

"You mean you're working on it all alone?"

"Yes."

"You absolutely have not farmed it out anywhere for testing, like you've sometimes done?"

"No."

"You know what I'm thinking, don't you?" I asked in a subdued voice, after a pause.

Sam's answer, after an even longer pause, was also yes.

"That clears up a lot," Josh said briskly after the call was disconnected. "Obviously, *somebody* has his hands on the gizmo, whether Sam's aware of it or not."

"Mike," I said instantly.

"Maybe. Sam trusts him absolutely, and the guy's a tinkerer. But there's still no way he could have stolen the game programs. Not even the one I was stupid enough to play for him," Tracy said.

She sounded as if she wanted that to be true. Josh looked disgusted, but I understood and I ached for her. Mike was a heel, and probably much, much worse, but all the same.

And Tracy was also hoping against hope that she hadn't unwittingly been an "accessory to the fact," as the police would say.

I spoke as gently as I could. "Yes, he could have. You played your game with him on the computer in this car, didn't you?"

"Yes, but —"

Josh suddenly let out a roar. "Of course! Sam *told* us this computer was a Gemini prototype with Samantha's special features! Samantha could steal anything from any place, anywhere, so long as she was within a few miles of the other data bank, or could network into it!"

Chapter 18

We were approaching Malibu now. "We can't check tire tracks in total darkness, and flashlights could arouse suspicion," Josh said, and told Tracy to pull in at the next rest stop.

The seats in the Mercedes folded down into what amounted to a king-sized bed. We slept huddled together like campers, Josh's arms around me. It was dawn when I felt him stirring. Tracy had already raised the driver's seat and stepped outside. We went into the rest stop restaurant and had breakfast with truckers who had also been sleeping in their vehicles.

Pale sunlight gilded the streets as we drove toward the beach in Malibu. I pulled out the printout with Mike's address, and had the car computer print me out a local road map. I watched it, and Josh watched the street signs, as Tracy drove. Malibu was not like the New Jersey beach towns I was familiar with. Houses and apartments were crowded close together and only occasionally, between them, could you catch glimpses of the sea. But the area we were in clearly had money in the air.

We found Mike's secret beach house, circled the block once, then pulled away. "We'd better not be conspicuous," Josh said. "Park in the first shopping center." We walked back, carrying cameras.

Clearly, Mike was in the process of setting himself up in the Kennedy and Tyler style. The beach house was driftwood-modern and surrounded by a wrought-iron fence.

But the gate was not locked. The carport, when we reached it cautiously, was empty.

Weary letdown was sweeping over me when Josh said suddenly, in a tight voice, "Webster, look here."

There was no car, but there were tire tracks. I whipped up my camera just as Josh was doing the same thing.

"There are more of the same tracks in the dirt along the edge of the garden strip," he said. "See the way the inner rim's worn down on the left tire?"

Tracy said nothing. She left the garage abruptly and went to stand at the edge of the embankment, staring down at the beach below. My heart ached for her, but there was nothing I could say that would make things better. *At least she knows now that it wasn't her brother who was involved*, I thought.

We still had to prove that to the police.

I turned back to my photography with a vengeance. When we had ample shots of both tire tracks and beach house, we went back to the Mercedes.

"I'll drive," Josh said firmly, shrewdly sizing up Tracy's state. Tracy did not protest when he took the keys. He sat in front, alone, and Tracy came in the back with me and the computer. "We'll take you home before we go to the police," Josh said, pulling out of the parking lot. "Someone has to be there to sign for those Express mail deliveries. And we still need to figure out where Kubiczek altered the *Numero Uno* disks. You didn't bring Samantha's case record disks with you, did you, Webster? I wonder if this car computer could come up with answers."

"Don't bother," I said, feeling sick. "I think I know. At SMN. If Mike's been using Samantha's twin, here, for dirty tricks, it would be a cinch for him to gain access to anything and anywhere in the SMN plant. Including that new secret invention Sam confirmed. He could alter Unicorn disks there, and send them out through the SMN shipping room, and then zap the records of it out afterwards. Nobody'd be any the wiser."

Josh nodded. "All we have to do is find proof of it."

"Sam will know how to. When we tell him." We all fell silent.

We were out of Malibu now, on a highway skirting Los Angeles and heading north. Sun dazzled on the Mercedes' hood. I leaned back against the caramel leather upholstery, feeling the automobile's contained power.

"I wonder what this car would be like without speed limits," I murmured giddily. And then, *"Josh! Look out!"*

A red car had come hurtling out of a concealed drive, causing Josh to veer sharply to the right. The other car surged ahead, then slowed.

The same thought struck all our minds.

"It can't be," I said stupidly.

"It is a Ferrari," Tracy said. "It's following us!"

"One way to find out," Josh muttered. He slowed the Mercedes, and the red car slowed also. We were unable to get a good look at the driver.

"We can't risk this." Josh stepped on the gas.

I snapped on the computer and the telephone, and commanded, "Find Jennifer."

Within minutes Jennifer was on the line. She had gone to the office early. Jeremy was still in jail. Had we found any evidence she could use? "Plenty," I said succinctly. "Can't talk now. Where is everybody?"

"Sam's at the hotel. I just talked to him. He said Hatch had just arrived. Mike? Still there, I guess. Sam didn't say. Why?"

"I can't explain. Get over there, round everybody up, and sit on them! And for heaven's sake, stop trying to get Jeremy out on bail! He's safer there!"

"Sidney, what's going on? Where are you?"

"I can't explain on the phone! Just stand by, and keep the press away! Maybe you'd better tell the district attorney you're going to have new evidence later in the day." I hung up before she could ask me any more questions.

The Ferrari was still in sight, a few cars away. There were several cars behind us now, and light traffic in the opposite direction. "Whoever it is can't do anything along here," Jeremy said. "If it's Mike —"

"Who else could it be?" Tracy asked bitterly. It was the first time she'd spoken.

"Hatch!" The name came to me automatically. I felt Josh react, then he nodded.

"We don't know. Hatch and Mike *could* be in this together. Whichever one's in that car, he'll make his move as soon as we're clear of traffic. Because if he's here, he knows we're onto him."

"How?" I demanded. Then I caught my breath. "Car phones operate on short wave frequencies, don't they, like radios? If Mike suspected something fishy — from the phone call Sam received, or the Mercedes being gone from the hotel lot — he may have tried to tune us in!"

"He'd know how." Tracy leaned forward, scanning the road intently. "Josh, I know this road. I've come down here with friends to surf. We're about to hit a stretch that's all sharp curves and a real bad drop-off. If Mike tries anything along here —"

She didn't need to finish. Josh and I had both seen plenty of TV car chases along the California coast.

As soon as we were out of the Ferrari's sight range around the next curve, Josh swung without warning into a concealed side road.

"I'm going to double round and circle back. Make sure your seat belts are buckled," Josh ordered, "and hang on!"

The telephone squawked.

"Don't answer it! It could be a trap!" Tracy shouted.

"We have to! It may be important." I lifted the receiver, snapped the amplifier on, but didn't say a word. I didn't have to. Jennifer's voice came through, crisp and tight.

"If this is who it should be, you know who I am. Ivan Hatch is under guard in the hospital intensive care unit. He went off a cliff on his way from the exhibit to the Unicorn plant. His brake lines were cut. He may not live." She rang off abruptly.

There was no longer any question of who was driving the red Ferrari. There was no doubt in my mind about who had tampered with Hatch's car. Josh, his face set, stepped on the gas.

Within minutes we were back on the main road. Within minutes the Ferrari appeared and was closing in.

"I have to get him off this road," Josh muttered, more to himself than us. There was less traffic now. Suddenly Josh swung directly across the road and up a sandy embankment that climbed high.

With a screech of brakes the Ferrari was after us. There were no marked lanes or road signs now. We careened madly, sending clouds of sand up from the dunes, and I hung on tight and prayed.

It felt like a TV rerun: hide and seek, drag race, car ramming car. Or it would have felt that way if it hadn't been for the sickening lurch all through my body as several tons of motorized metal slammed and slammed again at the door beside me. Involuntarily, humiliatingly, I cringed.

"Get your head down!" Josh yelled. After a moment he added in an undertone, "It's Mike. I can see him."

I crouched down as I'd been told and tried not to think.

"We're coming to a side pocket. I'll try to trap him." Josh slammed his foot down on the gas and shot ahead. I heard a roar as the Ferrari followed. Josh whipped the Mercedes around, back past the other car and to the left at a ninety-degree angle that threw me sideways and cut off Mike's escape.

It happened so fast, but it felt like slow motion. The car spun to one side. It stopped. Josh unbuckled my seat belt and shoved me to the floor. "Get down!"

"If you think you can —"

"Stay out of sight! We can't afford to have him grab you! You, too, Tracy! Webster, get on the bleeper and call the police." Josh opened his door just wide enough to slide out, and crouched down behind the car in one swift move.

I reached up and jammed the locks down on my door, grabbed the telephone, and got the operator and demanded the police.

Behind me, I heard the sound of a car door opening.

Still holding the receiver tightly, I spun around.

Tracy. Tracy was out of the car, out from all protection, deliberately walking toward the Ferrari as Mike climbed out of it, looking as though he could not believe his eyes.

Chapter 19

He had a gun in his hand. Tracy ignored it.

"You're insane," she said carefully.

Tracy stood her ground with contempt in every line of her slender body. Mike moved toward her slowly, his gun steady.

"I didn't want this," Mike said, almost apologetically. "I didn't want to hurt anybody. And I certainly didn't want to get you involved."

Shockingly, Tracy laughed. "Not involve me? When you put the make on me to get our game? It was you who doctored the *Numero Uno* disks, too, wasn't it? Using Sam Kennedy's secret new prototypes? After my brother got you the job with him, because he thought he'd fired you unfairly? He knew I could give you an alibi for the time he'd thought our game was stolen, but he didn't know you'd stolen it on the Mercedes' computer memory while you were in Sam's car making out with me! Feeding me the line about how *mature* I was, how *sensitive* I was, how I *inspired* you!"

"It was no line."

"I suppose it was you who sent the doctored disk to Shuttleworth, too, and tipped off the police back east?"

I realized suddenly what she was doing. She was drawing Mike out, slowing him down, giving him a chance to hang himself in our hearing — and Josh a chance to sneak up if he could. I sensed, rather than saw, Josh's cautious move.

"No!" Mike was saying, outraged. "I had nothing to do with Shuttleworth! That was Ellerbee's doing! He found out about the gambling and thought he could cash in."

"Is that why you killed him?" Tracy taunted. "Because you didn't have the guts to face the consequences? It takes less nerve to set off a bomb by remote control than to meet a threat face-to-face, doesn't it?"

With a sickening jolt I realized Tracy didn't know the full details of how Ellerbee had been killed.

"I didn't plan to!" Mike shouted. "I didn't plan for you to be there when the bomb went off! Nobody was supposed to get hurt! Your brother could have collected on insurance. But you got there early — and Ellerbee found out about the phone call, and got there first. He threatened to turn me over to the police if we didn't cut him in on the gambling deal, so I had to —"

All at once, Tracy got it. I could tell by the

tensing of her body. "So you killed him deliberately?" she asked softly. "You cut the
lines on Hatch's brakes, too, didn't you? Was
he the 'we' you referred to? What happened,
Mike? Did he get greedy? Did you find out
the big guys weren't as easy to get rid of as
a dazzled girl?"

Almost unnoticeably, her foot moved a step
forward, toward him. I reached for the car
door lock.

The phone receiver squawked.

Tracy took a second step. Mike's gun
shifted.

"Police station. Sergeant Dreyfus. Are you
there? *Hello*?"

I shouted into the phone our approximate
location and that we were in dire need of
assistance.

Tracy took another step.

"Get back!" Mike's voice came like a whip
crack. "I don't want to, but I don't have anything to lose —"

Tracy's foot suddenly kicked sand up, out
toward his face. She threw herself to the
ground, and Josh sprang.

Have I mentioned before this that Josh is
an aficionado of the martial arts? I don't
know what particular Bruce Lee trick he'd
uncorked this time, but when the dust had
cleared I beheld a satisfying sight. Josh had
Mike well in hand — not in the classic legs-
spread arms-against-the-car position, but in
something out of a Kung Fu movie. Tracy
had the gun and was holding it at Mike's

head, and Mike's arm was twisted unbeliev-
ably and was being twisted more.

"Bring handcuffs, and maybe an ambulance," I told the telephone, noting the blood
and bruises on everybody's faces.

The sergeant wanted to know what charges
we'd be pressing.

"Try grand theft auto and attempted
murder for openers," I said crisply. I hung
up, and got out of the car to listen to Mike
sing.

Yes, he'd hit Jeremy's Jag a few times the
other night. The visibility had stunk and the
road was slippery, that was all. Yes, he owned
a Ferrari and a beach house; what was wrong
with that? Yes, he'd sold a game to Unicorn's
major competitor while he was still employed
by Unicorn, but so what? It was his game,
and if Tracy tried to say it was hers, well,
that was just because she'd had a crush on
him and wanted to get even when he'd
thought she was too much of a kid.

"Not good enough," Josh said, and rolled
him over so his face was in the sand. Josh
applied an interesting hammerlock and ex-
tracted the admission — this time in front of
Tracy and me as witnesses — that yes, Mike
had stolen Jeremy and Tracy's game and sold
it.

"Now, about the bomb and Ellerbee's
murder," Josh demanded.

At that moment the police arrived.

That was the end of Mike's "cooperation."
He started threatening to file charges of

assault and battery, and demanded to see his lawyer.

"It won't be Ms. Kennedy. She's representing Jeremy Tyler and Unicorn," I told him coldly.

We all had to go to the police station to make statements. As soon as we mentioned the Unicorn case, everybody snapped to attention. A lieutenant telephoned the Palo Alto police, and after that we were not only free to leave, we were practically thrown out.

We went across the street to a fast food place and it was there Josh and I squeezed into a booth and I telephoned Jennifer to tell her what had happened.

When I had finished there was a momentary silence. "Do you know," Jennifer said at last, "I'm not surprised. Mike's been a good hanger-on for Sam, but I've never felt comfortable about him, somehow. Maybe it's because I remembered how he put the make on Tracy a while back. She fell for him like a ton of bricks, and that worried me. But then she ditched him, and I breathed a sigh of relief."

"I feel bad for Sam," I said.

"Sam," Jennifer retorted, "will be so relieved Jeremy's cleared that all he'll feel for Mike now is cold, cold anger. I'll break the news to him, so he can start looking for evidence of how Mike used SMN equipment for doctoring the games. You can tell Sam the full story when you get here. Right now I want to get to the police station and demand my client be released. By the way, Hatch is going to pull through."

Then we were back in the car, heading north toward Silicon Valley, and this time no one followed. Tracy, in the back seat, was wrapped in silence, her eyes closed. I leaned against Josh's shoulder as he drove a legal fifty-five and thought longingly of a swimming pool or the Jacuzzi.

"We still have loose ends to tie up." Josh read my mind. "Once Mike gets a lawyer he'll either shut up entirely or deny everything we heard him say."

"We have the tire tracks. And he's the only person who could have rigged *Numero Uno*."

"*Sam* could have. Sure we know he didn't, but the Gemini prototype and the new gizmo are Sam's babies, after all. The tire tracks don't prove attempted murder. Mike will admit to stealing the other game and selling it to a competitor. He'll claim that because of that little deal, he didn't *need* the *Numero Uno* gambling rip-off to make him rich."

"You mean we need proof he was involved with gamblers. And proof he used SMN equipment to doctor the *Numero Uno* games."

"Sam and Samantha can prove the computer part," Josh said. "But that will just mean where and how the doctoring was done. It won't prove *Mike* did it, and sold the game disks to the syndicate. He was paid off in cash, remember? His Las Vegas charge records don't prove he had contact with the syndicate while he was there!"

We reached the Tyler condo, and as soon as we started up the steps, the door flew open.

"Jeremy!" Tracy catapulted into her brother's arms and then — now that the danger was all over — went to pieces. I felt like doing it, too, but Josh's arm was around me, supporting me. And our work wasn't over.

We sat down with Jeremy, and Sam and Jennifer, who were there, too, and recounted the whole story. Not only what had happened in Malibu, but all our hacking, and the conclusions to which it had led us.

"If you'd only told me you'd played the prototype game with Kubiczek," Jeremy said to Tracy, bleakly, and Tracy said, "I *know!* But I didn't want you to know I'd been such a fool . . . and I didn't see any way he could have stolen it. I didn't know about that computer's memory."

"If you'd told your brother, and he'd told his lawyer . . ." Jennifer said pointedly. *"I* knew about the Gemini prototype in the Mercedes."

She didn't finish the statement. If all those things had happened, *Numero Uno* might never have been tampered with. The Advocates for Children would not have been dragged in. A bomb would not have gone off, and a man would not be dead.

I told Jeremy about my conversation with Aldous P. Shuttleworth, and Jeremy nodded. "Maybe I can get him to work with me on getting stiffer laws against computer game piracy. He means well, and he has a good organization. . . . I think what we need right now is a dip in the Jacuzzi. We're all aching from lack of sleep."

That wasn't all we were aching from, I thought, remembering Josh's hammerlocks that were all that had held Mike till the police arrived. We went to the dressing rooms, and put on suits, and were just descending into soothing bubbles when the doorbell rang.

"I'll go," I said, pulling on a robe.

I found a mailman on the doorstep with an Express mail package for me from Cordelia. I signed for it with shaking fingers.

Inside were the materials Ceegee'd promised he'd have her send, plus a pile of photographs he'd gotten somehow from one of the computer magazines. Photographs that were, like the tape from the TV station, "outtakes."

I spread them out on the coffee table, and all of a sudden a scene leaped out at me. Mike, looking every inch the Malibu swinger — carefully combed hair, open shirt, gold chains — sitting at a hotel lounge table with Ivan Hatch and a couple of other men whose faces were very familiar from recent TV news shows. They were the gamblers who were being investigated for their illegal use of Unicorn's games.

There were printouts on the cocktail table in front of them. There was even a sign on an easel in the background, announcing the well-known singer who was appearing nightly in the hotel lounge. The date was some six months ago — two months before the rumors of Unicorn's gambling tie-in.

Holding the picture carefully, I went out to the hot tub and eased myself down onto the ledge. "Here's that hard evidence you wanted," I said to Josh demurely.

Jeremy snatched the picture from me and took a good hard look. Then he let out a whoop and passed it to Jennifer.

In two seconds Jeremy and Jennifer were out of the tub and on the phone, telling the police that they were on their way. Tracy and Sam went with them. Josh and I did not, for we were otherwise engaged.

The case ended as it had begun — in what Cordelia would no doubt call a "passionate clinch." (From my perspective, who needs names? Just enjoy!) Only this time, being in California, it had a touch of madness.

When you kiss in a Jacuzzi, the bubbles tickle your nose.

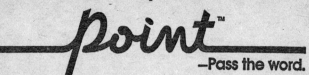